TIME'S COVENANT

ERIC ORMSBY

TIME'S COVENANT

SELECTED POEMS

BIBLIOASIS

Copyright © 2007, Eric Ormsby

FIRST EDITION

Library and Archives Canada Cataloguing in Publication

Ormsby, Eric L. (Eric Linn), 1941–
    Time's covenant : selected poems / Eric Ormsby.

ISBN 978-1-897231-21-0 (CASED)
ISBN 978-1-897231-20-3 (PBK.)

    I. Title.

PS8579.R58T54 2007   C811'.54   C2006-904687-5

Canada Council   Conseil des Arts
for the Arts   du Canada

We acknowledge the support of the Canada Council for the Arts for our publishing program.

PRINTED AND BOUND IN CANADA

For Daniel and Charles

dear sons

CONTENTS

Coastlines (1992)

1: A Florida Childhood

2: The Way North

For A Modest God (1997)

I.

Araby (2001)

Daybreak at the Straits (2004)

Uncollected Poems (1958-2006)

Time's Covenant

PREFACE

This selection contains the five books of poems I have published to date together with a smaller assortment of new and uncollected poems from books still in progress. The earliest poem here dates from 1958, the most recent from 2006. The book therefore has a fair claim to be representative of my work in verse over almost half a century. The arrangement is chronological by collection, though that may be misleading since all five collections have included poems written ten or fifteen years prior to publication. When I put together a selection in 1997, I excluded a number of poems from my first two collections. Some of these I have restored; I like them better now than I did then. I've removed several poems from the later collections, and have tinkered here and there with many of those which remain.

The poems in "Time's Covenant," the final section, represent a sample from a long collection which I have been working on for a number of years. Covenant itself is a fictional recreation of a 19th-century Utopian community in Tennessee, based on a similar settlement where my grandmother and her sisters and brother grew up; it bears no factual correspondence, beyond a few names, to the actual place. Certain poems in earlier collections, such as "Dicie Fletcher" and "The Suitors of my Grandmother's Youth," also form part of this larger book, which is still in progress.

In assembling this selection, as in the writing of the poems themselves, I have benefited continually from the attentive eye, unerring taste and elegant sense of style of my wife Irena. She has rescued me, again and again, from my own worst tendencies; if these have persisted, despite her best efforts, my own stubbornness is to blame. Her love and her constant encouragement have sustained me throughout.

I

BAVARIAN SHRINE

In memory of Paul R. Hoffmann

"Only curving praise of rain
lifts the still gesture into green."

—Paul R. Hoffmann, "The Snail of Trees"

Starfish

The stellar sea-crawler, maw
Concealed beneath, with offerings of
Prismed crimson now darkened, now like
The smile of slag, a thing made rosy
As poured ingots, or suddenly dimmed—

I appreciate the studious labour
Of your rednesses, the scholarly fragrance
Of your sex. To mirror tidal drifts
The light ripples across or to enhance darkness
With palpable tinctures, dense as salt.

You crumple like a puppet's fist
Or erect, bristling, your tender luring barbs.
Casual abandon, like a dropped fawn glove.
Tensile symmetries, like a hawk's claw.

You clutch the seafloor.

You taste what has fallen.

Lazarus in Skins

After his long recovery, Lazarus
Began wearing lizard-skin boots.
He sported cravats of rich kid
And black lustrous jackets of young calf.
He couldn't endure the cling
Of fabric, the insinuations of silk.
Even textiles woven of moth-soft cloth
Aggravated his dreams.

Not suffering, he said, but hope
Had made him hysterical and vain.
Now he desired the sinuous
Space of other skins, those fresh
Folds of amplitude, the beautiful
Blueness of snakes' eyes, cloud
Lenses, when they shed their last skin.

Railyard in Winter

The colours of disused railyards in winter;
the unnamed shades of iron at four o'clock;
the sun's curiosity along abraded stones;
corrosion that mimes the speckled lichen of woods;
the islands of stubbly rust on padlocked doors;
the fierce shoots of winter grass among cinders;
the fragile dim light, infused with tannin,
that falls clear on the stamped bottle-glass
and regales the castoff boot.

                            The colours of shale
cratered with dark rain. The rough knots
of crabgrass near the steps to the loading dock
and their sandy scruffed umber.

                            The hues
of all negligible things: the nugatory blue
of slagchunks between the ties. Then, the smell
of those resinous blisters of red on the fence,
like a childhood of pines.

                            Such unpeopled places
luxuriate on Sundays. What was made for use
discloses in uselessness its transient magic;
assumes the radiance of the useless grasses.

Bavarian Shrine

In memory of Albert E. Flemming

1

The rusted feet of Christ in roadside shrines
Where the eager nail has bled into the stone
Transform the tough-hewn birch that disciplines.

His agony is fossilized in red
Lichens of corrosion on pale linden wood.

The oldtime craftsmen carved Him like a goose
With slathered ribs that spew out lymph and pus;
Three lurid ulcers colonize His thigh;
Pustules of malachite surround each eye.
A loving laceration smears His mouth.
Affection and the brute regard for truth
Suture His temples with the maggot's twist.
The black iron spikes surge from His wrists.

And yet, for me, this victim, tethered like
A swan, is lewd and holy:
                                    O Thou
Peacock of decay . . .

2

The spotted hogs trot past to the abattoir.
Their flanks are mired with fear-dung, and they squeal.
Their pink noses snuffle the poignant air.
Men club the hogs with black padded hammers,
Then swing them up on hooks and stab their throats.
Their shrieks are inconsolable and mad.
Their eerie voices give the shrine its cry.
Pilgrim, you shudder, stung by hurt and fear.

The thighs of Christ are burnished and severe.
A murderous perfection lights His eye.

A downy princess texture to the skin
—Only the exquisite can savour pain—
The royal exclamations of a flame
That feeds most fiercely on the tutored nerve.
Aristocratic in His gilded Calvary
—Did the numb peasants worship in His form
The hated bodies of their feudal lords,
Imagining beneath the ermine cloaks
Flesh that could whimper to the flail's white strokes?

3

The pretty little hogs with spotted sides,
Their fern-like ears scrolled over clever eyes,
That pick a delicate path on trotting hooves
Across the trash and mud of a weathered sty,
Enthralled me as I knelt beside the shrine.
(I share the German fondness for their swine.)

In autumn, when they come to butcher them, I
Memorize their long, despairing squeals
That fill the Bauernhof. I smell their blood,
The stink of singeing bristle and the smoke,
But feel the most for those that cannot cry,
Who wedge their frightened bodies to the fence
And shake with dumb-struck terror, paralysed
And staring, or expel quick spurts of nervous dung
That stains their patterned haunches and stiff tails.

And afterwards, just past the killing-ground,
I watched a hunting spider trap the flies
Invited by the reek of thickened blood;
Her dust-embedded web only an instrument,
All wonder butchered, pure function manifest,
With jags of dark heart's blood snagged on the strands.

Forgetful Lazarus

Lazarus forgot his gloves and the blots
On his numb fingers showed too white.
He forgot the injustices of his shoes,
The lichens on his toes began to glow.
Lazarus could not remember to cover his mouth,
The grey smell of his entombment coiled out.

He also forgot his skyblue-tinted lenses
That made his sunken eyeballs shine with life.
He forgot to scrape away his death
That laced his arms and legs, his cheeks
—vivid and difficult as the rose-rich gills of fish—
with delicate ruffles of fungus, with sweet mould.

Cover the Statues

Dominica passionis

This purple has the squalor of neglected gardens,
Root-refuse, the scabrous reek of cabbage,
Or the horrifying sundown-violet of bruises
On bedsore thighs, that crawling decay of the blood
That rises along the fingernails.

This purple has the cast of shame,
The radical lavender of humiliation,
That cloaks the startled skin in the dour
Spotlights of interrogation, that almost bluish shade
Of frightened nakedness, those cobalt
Demarcations of the groin and armpits.

This purple that first shows
Around my eyes after certain broken nights,
This stiff surplice of grief,
This shrewd chasuble of disenchantment,
This flickering procession of mourning:
Purple candleflames borne over grey plazas
In the final daylight.

This purple that seems almost to chime
To the waking senses of the bees.

Lazarus and Basements

Lazarus had been a sluggish kid,
Fond of musky crevices where moles
Doze or where opossums paw their sour
Disreputable nests. He loved
That asylum of old clothes where moths
Webbed the spotted lightbulb or the crawl
Cellar where the fat exterminator went
On his monthly trips.

                At night he saw
Spiders in his sleep and dream itself
Furled outward in tough silk from the sly
Spinnerets of sleep. When he died,
They planted him in a damp and mildewed hole.
His basement nature had come home at last.

Imagine our surprise
Not at his wet, still-bandaged face
By the grave's low door,
Nor at the rank and vicious stink
That smoked from his shroud,
But at his loving familiarity with the damp
And the companionable clasp of his arms
Brimming with vermin
And all the grey caresses of his twittering friends.

Fetish

After we came home from the Exhibition,
I felt drawn to make a figure out of wood.
I took a bulgy anonymous chunk, with bark
Attached and gummy tears near the frequent knots.
First I hacked and chopped; an anger
Somehow welled up, impelled my hands.
But the rough bristling form emerged:

Its hands were fingerless fists,
Its feet were lopped blocks.
Gently I gouged its bellybutton out and then
The face took its terrible shape—
That knobby lumb of grieving watchfulness.
I suggested breasts and nipples
With red pegs. But then, as though instructed,
I modelled a fierce priapic flare,
Instinct with secret seed, double as snail-sex.

But the mouth's awe
Oppressed me—that torn place that prayed . . .
Upstairs I heard dinner and the gameshows begin.
Beyond the basement windows, rain prepared.
I had before me such a crooked god
Huge in the spotted bulb. So I took nails,
The shiny wide-head wood-nails from a keg,
And drove them skreaking home. Each spike
Increased its light, each hammer blow spilled
Adoration on the hunching thing, and I
—I knelt down before it while my lips burned.

My fetish swelled against its blinking nails,
Assumed a crabbed magnificence: *My pain had form.*
Its chopped mouth mirrored darkness: cascades
Of mirrors reflected an infinitude of dark,
Night within multiple night.

And then it spoke:

With upheld beggar's stumps *Bend down*, it said,

> *Bend down*
>> *And cherish me*!

Lazarus in Sumatra

> "But what thinks Lazarus? Can he warm his blue hands
> by holding them up to the grand northern lights? Would
> not Lazarus rather be in Sumatra than here?"
> —Melville, *Moby Dick*

I wanted to warm his blue hands,
I tried to rub the life back
Into his flat cheeks, his slack jaw.
See, I whispered, the sun
Abrades the rippled roof
And strops his coroner's claws
Against the rain . . .
Did I want to shock him back
To life, with all its imprecations?

The ground is damp and sandy;
Graves are scooped out of dunes.
The strict sun does not revive
But desiccates all that it falls across:
I felt him toughen, turn stringy.

He was a thing out of place
In that simulacrum of paradise
Like the skull of a doll.

He was so windshorn, so weatherbent,
He had become such drift,
Such plangent bone,
His complexion the stark of chalk.

Death, here,
Means curling back into that
Simplicity of shape
—S-curve, nascent parabola,
The little elipses of the bones—
Corrective to the sun's extravagance:

A loyalty to one's own first dimensions.

Rites de Passage

After we buried our Grandmother
In the western corner of the basement,
We began to understand new names
For silences, but they were disturbing:
There were names that made us jump
Like *sfeegkx*! or *broasfi!*
Or names that produced a chill sweat at night
Like *ukkakk* or *qiz'raf.*
But then, the names of those stillnesses
Attracted us also. We had never known
That silences could be so divisible and soft
Or that they could glove our skins
In clinging expectancies, like the mute bronze
Pauses before and after the gongs . . .

In winter we realized that, after all,
Grandmother had mastered every voicelessness.
We came to understand how all our talk
Somewhere else reversed itself, like steep
Tunnels of speechlessness beneath our sounds.
Our conversations seemed tinny with echoes,
Even our whispers had a gauzy clang,
Even our cries of love rang woozy as saws.

We felt some implacable intellect at work
More powerful than all our grandmothers.

In late July we exhumed them, one by one.
With eyes averted and with fervid prayer
We consecrated all the eastern walls.

Now our speech has regained its ancient symmetry.

Lazarus Listens

The relentless waltzes of the Golden Age
Retirement Club upstairs left him no peace.
All night their scything strings rippled his nerves,
Attuned to spider-sighs and beetle-whisperings.
All night he heard parades
And festivals, fiestas where rude shoes
Finessed their sad mazurkas into dawn.
And then, at dawn he heard the pure
Arpeggios of hooligans in stairwells
Or his ears, pitched
To the yawns of moths,
Followed the thin, self-conscious lullabies
Of senile women in their flowered chairs,
Cradling the surprise of light.

He was inert as earth,
Simple as sand, consummate as clay,
The driest obstacle, the echo-nest,
Against which all their music dumbly beat.

Skunk Cabbage

The skunk cabbage with its smug and opulent smell
Opens in plump magnificence near the edge
Of garbage-strewn canals, or you see its shape
Arise near the wet roots of the marsh.
How vigilant it looks with its glossy leaves
Parted to disclose its bruised insides,
That troubled purple of its blossom!

It always seemed so squat, dumpy and rank,
A noxious efflorescence of the swamp,
Until I got down low and looked at it.

Now I search out its blunt totemic shape
And bow when I see its outer stalks
Drawn aside, like the frilly curtains of the ark,
For the foul magenta of its gorgeous heart.

Foundry

Beyond the abandoned foundry
The ground of the dried-up creek
Is littered with blue chunks of slag.
Sometimes you spot a snake,
Dry as those glassy fragments,
Sliding among the refuse heaps
But shiny as unexpected water,
Where everything in July is parched and white.

I cherish the curls and brusque escarpments
Of what was lopped and pared
From cooling pig-iron on the hissing floor
A hundred years back
—those gritty amethysts of slag.

In the shade of the casting house
I worked a handwrought nail
Out of a powdery corner.
Delicate flakes of corrosion
Brightened my fingertips.
The air had the taste of old
Iron reddened by the dryness of time.
In its harsh twist
The nail gave back
The heat and labour of its forging
Like fierce light from long-dead stars.

Moths at Nightfall

The moths alarmed us.
They were big and dark and they clung
Against the screen at night
Like starving children.
They were intent on the light
Inside and afterwards, the banal
Lamps seemed marvellous in our eyes:
For hours, Grandma's cherished table lamp
With its pink silk shade
Glowed against their darkness
Like a signal fire.

                   The moths'
eyes had a slick black glitter
In the inaccessible brightness of parlours.
Their madras wings, graced
With a dusty haze of pollen,
Pulsed so slowly upon the screen
All night. And their stark
Delicacy of fringed and pluming
Antennae, keen to the most
Distant perfumes, enthralled
And repelled: they curved like white
Ferns banished from the daylight,
Or sometimes, as we watched them,
Their feathery antennae furled outward
And seemed to tremble with attention,
Vivid against the darkened yard beyond.

Precious Vials

She kept her room darkened against a sun
That fades and ages things. I liked to slip
Inside while she napped, or on those afternoons
She disappeared into the beery dusk
Of the Everglades Bar & Grill, I'd hide in there
Behind the dresser, or poke through her desk.
Outside, the loud stucco houses fumed in the damp
Miami glare. Inside, her cashmere shawls, from cooler climes,
Lay leaved in crackling tissue on cedar shelves.
A noble caravan of ivory animals
Mounted her chiffereau, all gently yellowed
Where some excluded light had struck. Old
Velvets insisted on being felt. Alarming
Silks rippled my ignorant fingers. But most mysterious,
There stood before the mirror in her room
A throng of vials and iridescent flasks.

Within them amber fragrances lay coiled
Lazy as copperheads, or they doled a sullen shine
The way a woman's hair gleams
When she combs it back in a twilit room. "These are
My precious treasures," she would say,
"My precious vials of perfume, from all my beaux."
Ceremoniously she'd draw one dense
Pearl-coloured stopper and anoint
The insides of my wrists with a quick cold dab.
When the fragrance rose in my face I shivered.
There was a scent of springtime
And of crushed petals around us both
As though she'd drawn me in
Under her warm, still-drowsy gown,
Skin against skin.
"You are my precious treasure," she would say.

One night when the steep light sank
Back under the chalky stones of the yard, and I

Could prowl the darkened house, a spy,
An Indian scout, immersed in the secret
Friendliness of night, a blind cave-creature
In its sheltering stream, I heard
Noises outside. I snapped
The backyard floodlight on. She was
Sprawled in the grass of the yard, tangled
In the hug of somebody who wore a bright red
Baseball cap across his grey old skull.
"Jesus, sweetie pie," she groaned at me.
In the wincing light the whiteness
Of her legs frightened me.

The next day I stayed far
From her room. I felt
How all her treasures had begun
To tarnish in unwelcome light.
How the fine shawls disclosed
A raggedness of moths, how the ivory animals limped,
Disfigured as plastic left in the noonday sun,
How the precious bottles showed their clumsy seams
—mere factory casts!—running up their backs
Like a wind-stunned thread of tears.

With bitterness I called to mind
How around each cloudy rim
Of her perfume bottles, where the inner glass
Gritted the fingertips like sand, I had seen
A residue of silt
—One of those little marks of age or use
That shames you later to recall
For your unforgiving eye: a smudged
And clotted imprint on the mouths
Of the bottles where the scent had
Evaporated, leaving only
Drab distillations behind, like a scar.

Wood Fungus

juts in grey hemispheres like a horse's lip
from tree-trunks. The outer edge is crimped
in sandy ripples and resembles surf.
The upper plane of the fungus does not shine
but is studious beige and dun, the hue
of shoe-soles or the undersides of pipes.

Jawbone-shaped, inert as moons, neutral
entablatures, they apron bark and pool
rain. Underneath they're darker, fibrous
and shagged.

        Mountain artists like to etch
intricate patterns on their flat matte skins
and their tobacco-bright sketch-marks look burnt
as tattoos or tribal tangles of scars.

When you grip their surfaces, they bruise.
When you pry them from their chosen oak,
they seem shut fast, like the eyes of sleepers,
or the tensed eyelids of children when they're scared.

Bee Balm

Their dusty spires of blossom look washed out,
Topple to the touch, a bone-pale lavender.
But monarchs flutter them, and fat bees
Tumble into their bleak intoxicating blooms.
On August mornings you will find the bees
Half-dead with feeding on the dizzy stems.
They grip their flowers in a love-clutch, feet
Enlaced, their black metallic eyes dulled with balm.
The tall chalky petals drip with them.
When the sun comes they twitch and shudder awake.
To us the scent is hot and mordant, prompts
Sneezes. To bees it is sweeter than home.
All night they cling sybaritic as pashas,
Their stiff golden fur dampened with pleasure.

Lichens

Between the stones, by the sea's edge,
And in sheltered hollows of the rock,
Flat lichens cling. Their surfaces are grey,
Dry and crinkly. Some are cracked and sharp
Or flake away like weathered paint in strips.
They survive the cold light and the spray
Torn from the North Atlantic. The way they clasp
And cover the rocks seems to signify
Inconspicuous courage and tenacity. But
At evening they gleam bleakly in exact
Configurations and their order is fiercer
Than the sea's: their drab arabesques
Look splotchy, rust-wept or scaly as dead bark;
Far-off they're starlike, spiky as galaxies.
Like us they clutch and grip their chilly homes
And the wind defines their possibilities.

Spiders

1

I caught a spider sucking a drink
From the kitchen sponge. Its thirst
Disgusted me. I didn't want to know
How our requirements coincide.

Still, it was almost beautiful
As the spider stepped from the wet sponge
And swung into the pot of mint,
Where I knew
It would rest and hide and savour
The cool taste of water
In its dark mouth.

2

Imagine my spider life
Woven in angles of dark.
A stray fly blunders to death
Next door. Majestic, my wife
Has launched her huge ark
Of strands, alive to the least breath
Of light and sequined with the wings
Of her feasting. Her repose is big.
The future winter glitters.

3

When I drew the last volume
Of the *Oeuvres* of Malebranche
From its snug slipcase, I
Found the broken egg-
Sack of a spider
Woven across the inner
Edges of the pages.
Since I last read the philosopher
(That fit of anxiety in May?)
A mother spider had sought out
His sheltering obscurity.

Did some fortunate affinity
Watch over her careful course?
I like to think that she valued the cold
Delicate structures of his mind;
For she knew in her
Belly what he meant when he
Wrote: "Error
Is the cause
Of man's misery"

—And of spiders' too.

Statues and Mannequins

1

The populous bronzes of our city
Doze greenly as winter draws on.
History topples in inconspicuous
Atoms of displacement—oh slowly, by
Schedules nestled in the foundry's
Neglected archives.

                                But the mannequins
Sport perfect cream-tinted breasts
And alluring alcoves of thigh,
And they gesture sandily in a time
Inaccessible to us—their eyes, how
Their eyes appear to seek shape
And finality, as though their designer
Impressed them with the jocular blessing
Of his consummate thumb.

                               Incorruptible,
Unseasonal, their vivid shades drift
Glibly, unscarred by the bright corrosions
Statues shoulder in their dying greenery.

2

From the twirled labyrinth of the finger
Print, enigmatic as a ritual bronze
Vessel (the massive purity of a Shang ewer
With its hieratic tiger's face), the sheer
Ethereal vectors of their lives appear.
The anonymity of night has coronated them.
A namelessness as lustral as the dawn
Invests them in sepals of nobility,
Vivifying, quick, acclamatory—

But these are brittle with the temporary,
Accommodate the sea-flash torn from cloud,
Gather their adoration in the sundown hour
When snowflakes batten on the iron lamps,
And have the lacquered isinglass of hurt
All negligible surfaces collect.

3

Because I loved their statuesque and votive
Stances, mere palettes for the stern couturier,
I graced their monochrome with mental
Harpstrings, grotesque in their slender
Melodies, and let imagination venerate
The classic shadows of their chins and ears.
The postures of mannequins are gossamer
While the heavy haunches of the monuments
Clutch cement and hunker down for ice.

All that dreaded life in me admired
The serene sterility of mannequins.
All that evaded love in me preferred
Their oratorical instant to the dim
Encumbrances of November and the slow
Disfigurement of moments that wear down
The willed fragility of all our monuments.

4

There is another world beneath the eyes
Of statues, where horizons hold
The drowsy verdegris of disenchantment.
There is another life in the open hands
Of triumph with its blind stigmata of rust.
The biting rain of late November
Corrodes their falcon pupils, lenses
Trained on essences.

                    Behind snug glass,
In the pampered habitats of mannequins,
The smarting contortions of the seasons
Appear as captivating as cascades.
The ornamental fountains of decay
That blush the momentary fingertips
With coral-shadows, sea-suffusions,
Gentle the imagination.

                    Mannequins betray
The patriarchal eyelids of the snow.

5

The lost gesture of the statue, that
Hesitation in glory, what ran from our
Fingers in the plazas of remembrance
—Sometimes, even here, where the sour
Winter circles, there is a fragrance
Of the sea conveyed by the grieving
Stones from the matrix of their origin
Or an iron wind offers the smell of the sea
From the east.

              Why were the works
Of our hands brittle as November,
Fugitive as the sparse light that falls
Over houses crouched against the cold?
Sometimes when the shrill silver
Of a moon sounds its bitter voluntary,
We feel it all along our skin,
Our shoulders assume that momentary
Majesty of tremulous codices, that
Piquant surface of the temporary
Skin, inscribed by the vivid light.

—Montreal, November 1989

December

December rings in the chill mouths of bells,
The shadowy solicitude of grasses
Eyelashed with precarious snow.
There is a crystalline insistence in the black
Repetitious roof-tops with their shock
Of snow. The ragged chimneys seem
To pray with fingers pinched
Together in entreaty while the luscious
Clouds of winter wallow on grey
Organzas of sundown.

                December bows
Under threadbare memories. The spider
In the corners of the house shrivels
To a small, dark claw. At night
Our dreams infringe and pool,
Our common terrors shake us in sleep.

Upriver there are remote
Oceans whose cold waves still ring
Like freezing echoes in the mouths of bells.

Craneworld

When the sandhill crane resolves
To hatch her universe, emphatic
Designs impose on her angle of view.
Her innate notions are splashy but few.
The blueprint of craneworld involves
Thatchiness, a prickledom of aromatic
Nestnesses. It is spatulate and concave
Together, and is conspicuous in fish.

In craneworld the sun is both god and slave
And the night rises in the darkness of the eye
Itself.

      Frogs' voices console her cosmos lavish-
ly and there is the strong calendar of sky
Southward.

      Her inwardness is spherical, grit-white,
Concentric in its cadences, with gravities of light.

River Plants

1: White Waterlilies

The waterlilies have a jagged look,
Spiky as aloes or the blades of palms,
And yet, seem almost bridal in their whitenesses.
Within, a diffidence of faint
Saffron shows, like the first intimations
Of morning or that almost indiscernible
Gold of willows at the start of spring.

The waterlilies ride the detours and
Dead-ends of the river where the current
Stalls and pools. Their petals open rigidly
Like the lacquered eyelashes of dolls.
Beside them, their wide flat leaves
Wobble with disparate waterdrops that roll
Like puzzled mercury on terrazzo floors.
They seem so still, ethereal and virginal.
Their fragrance is cold and white as their blooms.
Only when you lean to look within
Will you see the avid bees
Stagger in their yellow pollen.

2: Bullhead Lily

Like the sagging dial of a broken clock
The bullhead lily dangles its gold
Globular blossom above the stream.
The single flower bobs and wands on its
Resilient stem, right-angled to the crimped
Calm of its lily pad which seems to disavow
Its bold and nodding yellow, its bulbous
And insistent talon of petals.

The lily looks like a crab's eye on its stalk
Or a periscope probing upward from the mud
Or like a sceptre in a dozing hand.
But all such similes slide and fall away
Into the water where the lily grows
While its river-jostled shadow slants across
The cold circumference of its drifting leaves.

Once on a sandbar near a bend in the creek
I found a bullhead lily washed up in pale muck
And saw how its tubes of roots, spongy
And venous in the unaccustomed sun,
Assembled the mud, fisted its sufficiency
Of sand, as though its grip sustained
The shifting river darkness where it clung.

3: Pickerelweed

The sketchy stands of pickerelweed
That oversee the river's surface have
A lazy grace of curious alertness.
They seem to gaze away from shore
Especially in mid-summer when their small
Successive petals begin to form.

The newer blossoms continuously surmount
The dead and fading petals on the stem.
They sentinel the riverbank with scuffed
Steeples of attentive lavender
That show a bruised fluorescence as the day
Climbs. At noon the flowers pale,
Become inconspicuous, until the evening stream
Discloses a shading almost porphyry
In their ragged pinnacles.

                       At summer's end
The rhizome where their cool, slim stalks ascend
Coils in upon itself. Their leaves are marked
With calligraphic patterns of decay
Like the labyrinthine signatures
On ancient bronzes tarnished by the air.
There is a sense of stealth and
Supersession in the leaves.
After the frost has singed and stiffened them,
The leaves retract and curl, then crumple down
Like heirloom scarves that moths have spoiled.

Conch-Shell

1

The conch-shell on our kitchen counter leans
Sideways on its spiky, flaring lip,
Displaying a pinkish, petal-like interior.
The outer shell, much grittier,
Still has its papery membrane, a brown caul
Flaking away in tatters. This reminds us
That our shell is not mere ornament
But once housed some unappealing pale
Worm or slug-like being;
One of those slippery, spittle-
Mantled creatures who construct, laborious
In secretion, such begonia-plush
Palaces of glory.

Shells are paradoxical the way they draw
The eye, and then the fingertips, inside.
When we peek inside the conch-shell,
There is a sloping balustrade of faint
Pink before the darkness, almost like a bare
Shoulder glimpsed briefly in a window-frame.
When we look within, the final light
Dissolves in shadow, just as once we peered
Upward to where the staircase of our childhood
Spiralled into the dark.

2

The conch is the trumpet of solemn festivals
And its pinnacle—auger-threaded,
Spire-sleek, piquant as lance-
Tip or the brass casque of a khan—
Scalpels the roughened currents asunder.
But the russet life that hides inside,

Whose flesh tastes good in broths,
Flinches from the light.

The secret fabricator of itself,
Refusing to be known
By anything beyond the dawn-pink
Shell that houses and articulates
Its lithe inhabitant—
How that small crawling diffidence,
The slime-wreathed animal that flows,
A pygmy to its own magnificence,
Inches ocean runnels, seraphically akimbo!
This recluse with a flare for ostentation,
Glabrous and glistening, secure in glory
That it secretes but cannot see,
Emblems a self in its configuration.

3

I've seen conchs docked and husked,
Stripped of their calcareous splendour, plump
Amorphous things, arching, like tongues
Torn from mouths or some hidden
Shapelessness of desire drawn into the sun.
I've seen the unrecognizable architect
Of itself marketed in dripping baskets,
Leaving behind nothing but the pale
Pulsing of remembered oceans
In the veiled shell's proclamatory lip.

Fingernails

It is the patrimony of reptiles, or of birds,
To possess such pale claws, to sport such
Little flashes of keratin at the farthest tip
Of the grasp. The baby hoatzin has archaic
Claws along its barbarous wings
That boost it into the Peruvian trees;
So, too, our reminiscent hooks
That let our fingertips negotiate
The air, and that curve around so
Obediently, like shields at rest, with
All the snug patience of a carapace,
Snail's armature, or the fastidious
Hermit crab's limping pagoda of shell.

The manicurist lovingly rebukes
The creeping cuticle so that the faint
Crescents, like clouds along horizons,
Reappear. The fingernails are suffused
With the blood's sweet light
Though the nails of the newly dead
Possess a terrible hailstone
Opacity. The fingernails palisade
The unruly ranks of our wilful fingers
And whenever we clasp our hands,
A brief convivial darkness sheathes our nails.

Ears

Notwithstanding their cabbagy flanges,
These amiable extrusions of the sense
Have heraldic presences,
Are reminiscent on the bland
Expanses of our heads of those impossible
Imperial signatures the vain
Sultans affixed to their vellum
Promulgations.

                  The outer ear appears
Pure antechamber and accommodates
Embassies of echoes. How obediently
The hobnailed delegations of the heard
Vanish over satin lintels, only
To emerge inside transformed
By protocols of perception, like those crass
Vandals who come back from court
Tutored and articulate with significance.

It is the honour of the ears to serve
Opportunities for onyx or
The pearl's prerogatives because they curve
Reverent as harps before all sound and seem
Cambered like swans' wings for the vivid air.

Seen flat, the ears resemble riverbeds
Carved out by clever rivulets of sound:
Imagine what cadenzas pressed
Their vanishing remembrance on the flesh—
Not only the glissando of wind-squealing snow,
Shy appoggiaturas of the evening vireo,
But the percussive rasp of bleak
Gravel rattled, the triangular
Ping of rain in stony pails, reedy
Repetitions of the kitten's cry—

Imagine how, still shimmeringly, on
Tremulous tympani, vibrant
Within the ears, invisible
Petals of the voice arise.

Nose

The nose is antithetical. It sniffs,
Snuffles, wallows in sneezes, then recoils
In Roman nobility, profile-proud;
Pampers its fleshy shadow in bas
Reliefs or is serenely alcoved within
Rotundas where the chiselled light
Dapples its expansive flanges.

                              Nose
Is tuberous, root-like, with subsoil
Affinities, has its own mossy
Aromas, feels bulbous as corms or
Crimped as rhizomes; but even so,
Stands graced with little wings above
The harboured nostrils.

                    The nose
Sunders the face in symmetry,
Bisects us in hemispheres where selves
Negotiate along the boundary lines
Of smiles or scowls.

                    All night,
In the snug bed of the face,
The nose exults.

My Mother in Old Age

As my mother ages and becomes
Ever more fragile and precarious,
Her hands dwindle under her rings
And the freckled skin at her throat
Gathers in tender pleats like some startled fabric.
The blue translucence of her veins gives
The texture of her skin an agate gleam
And the dark-blue, almost indigo
Capillaries of her cheeks and forehead
Resemble the gentle roots
Of cuttings of violets
In sheltered jars.

              I love her now more urgently
Because there is an unfamiliar and relentless
Splendour in her face that terrifies me.

              "Oh, don't prettify decrepitude,"
She demands. "Don't lie!
Don't make old age seem so *ornamental*!"

And yet, she abets her metamorphosis,
Invests herself in voluminous costume
Jewels and shrill polyesters

                  —ambitious as a moth
To mime the dangerous leaf on which she rests.

II

COASTLINES

To the memory of my mother

Virginia H. Ormsby

Horseshoe Crab

She is surprising in her lowliness.
She follows the immemorial furrows
Along the tidal floor of the bay.
Her manufactured look disarms,
Brown as molded plastic or poured bronze.

The silt-dulled sheen of her carapace
Fits the hand despite thorny protrusions
Of chitin and that lacerating ice-pick
Of tail.

                    Underneath her frail rigidity,
Sculpted like the death-mask of a queen,
Her pale, segmented legs beckon and gleam.

My First Beach

It used to say *No Picnicking* in three
languages: in English and in Spanish and
in Yiddish. The Yiddish looked
spidery and mysterious. And on
the frond-green benches, in a
precious shade, fixed-income pensioners
from Jersey or Connecticut would chat
or doze. (Their poverty was hidden
but I'd heard grownup anecdotes of
cat-food suppers and of scavenging.)

Beyond their benches was the wall, a low
and plump-stoned wall of coral rock.
To me it meant that here the beach began.
Dim, indecisive waves lay just ahead.
Here there were picnics, here the tanned
paraded, muscular with oil, though now and then
you could spot pale newcomers with their
cuffs and collars still
stencilled on their unsunned skin.
I walked backwards to anticipate
the waves of my first beach which I could hear
sloshing behind me till they sounded like
the soapy buckets supers scattered down
Manhattan stoops, or tarpaulins upended
with taut rain. I walked backwards out of
loyalty to those old people whom I'd had to pass
before the seawall, as though by privilege
I owed them cognizance till out of sight.

But here, before the open waves, where beach
umbrellas bloomed in tulip rows, I had
the feeling that comes on you in a dream
of moving through some unfamiliar house
in August when the rooms are full of sun
and past each doorway you can glimpse

still further doorways bordered by a light
that has the spectral texture of your sleep,
is generous and almost palpable,
and even has a fragrance of its own,
warm and brightly drowsy, vanishing.

That was the dreamy feeling of my beach
that didn't last. For there I saw
the white-ribbed wavelets bundle to the shore,
like old men emptying their pockets out,
objects turned and smoothed for use,
if we still knew to use them—not
only sea-bottles darkened by the sun,
lost combs with swirls of seaweed in their teeth,
bones and obvious corals, brachiated
candlesticks of sponge and snarls of line,
but what I still could just identify:

tar-nuggets, terrible twists of wood, the arms of stars.

Remembrance

For Bruce

In dream sometimes there is the glamour of
an animal but afterwards,
alphabets emerge and people learn the monikers
reserved from all eternity for things.
The children are in love with etiquettes
but smell the sap inside the winter trees.
Old knuckles whiten on suspended porches.
You have the sense of sunlight where there move
figures of recollection wearing aprons and
a pair of vocal earrings, click of house-shoes,
the comfort of a long-anticipated sigh.

If only recollection could cohere! If only
memory were cogent once again!
The dispersed tatters of an ancient page
resume themselves in the curator's bath.
Or an old text, millennia-unread,
borrows coherence in a scholar's head.
Or as at nightfall once, above the Glades,
we witnessed ibises flap up and wheel
like scattered flocks of newsprint whipped by wind
that skim breeze-bellied on warm drafts of air—
a pandemonium of blank white wings,
spiky hysteria of hoots and swerves,
that steadily assembled into unisons
of swoops and slow encirclings, the loveliness
a single and concerted curve assumes
when many turn, and turn again, as one,
and so remembrance gathers islands up
and stitches estuaries to the gulf.

Adages of a Grandmother

Grandmother said to me, "Keep thyself
Unspotted from the world." She spoke in quotes.
I got the feeling that she had rehearsed
All her admonitions as a child,
For when she issued them to me she grew
Solemn and theatrical. I knew
She tasted in her words some sweet
Indissoluble flavour of the past; but even more,
As though at eighty-five or eighty-six
She stood still in the parlour of her recitation
—a plain, studious girl with long brown braids
(I have the portraits of her as a child)
—and spoke her lessons for approving guests.
Such touches of girlishness accompanied
Her adages. And then she gave me dimes
For so many lines of Shakespeare memorized.
For "The quality of mercy . . ." I was paid
A quarter, and at tea I gave her guests
A dollar's worth of Shakespeare with their toast.
"All the world's a stage," she reminded me.

Only armed with an adage might I sally forth.
"A foolish son's his mother's grief," she thought.
The world was scriptural and stratified.
It held raw veins of wisdom in its side,
Like the Appalachians when we journeyed north.
She sat in the front seat of the Buick, hair-net drawn
Over her white hair coiled in a dignified bun,
Her straw, beflowered hat alert and prim.
From the back seat I'd study her, my grim
Grandmother, with her dictatorial
Chin, her gold-rimmed spectacles ablaze with all
The glory of the common highway where
Field daisies spoke to her in doctrinaire
And confidential accents of the master plan
Confided to grandmothers by the Son of Man.

Wisdom was talismanic and opaque;
Could be carried in a child's small fist
Like the personal pebble I fished out of the lake.
And whenever I stepped outside she kissed
My head and armed me with a similitude.
Beyond the screen door, past the windowsill,
The bright earth rang with providence until
Even the wise ants at my shoe-tips moved
In dark amazements of exactitude
And the small dusty sparrows swooped innumerably.

I write this on the sun-porch of the house
Where she lay, an invalid, in her last years.
And I'm abashed to realize I blamed
Her stiffness and her stubborn uprightness
For much that happened to me afterward.
Now I look through the window where she looked
And see the sunlight on the windowsill
And wonder what it signifies,
For now I barely recognize
Her world outside, as though sunlight effaced
Not only human features but their memory.
Her adages are all scattered in my head
(*Neither a borrower nor a lender be*)
and I cannot think for thinking of the dead
(*Go to the ant, thou sluggard
consider her ways, and be wise.*)
I cannot read the world now with her eyes
(*A wise son maketh a glad father but
A foolish son is the heaviness of his mother!*)
And I, who used to blame her so,
Now rummage in my pockets for
A nickel's worth of wisdom for my kids.

Grackle

It's hard not to like the wise-
Guy grin, the almost sarcastic chatter
Of the boat-tailed grackle by the Everglades
Café. He has an acrid cackle,
A cacophony of slick and klaxon cries,
With tinsel whispers like a breathy flute.

His repertoire seems meant to flatter
Us by mimicry and so exonerate
Our grosser faults, our greeds,
Our clumsy cunnings, our minute
Duplicities.

               Watch how he hops elastically
From roof-beam down to a potato chip
And shrills and wheedles while his hard claws grip
Whittled bench-rims and the slats of rails.
He strides like a chimney sweep,
Char-coloured, and yet, see:
His cinder eyes are absolute.
Cunning of hunger makes his feathers bright
In smoky lapis, iris-indigo.

A Florida Childhood

The brick-red Spanish roof-tiles overlapped in patterns
Reminiscent of a snake's scales and the rainspouts held
Emaciated fingers to the soaking eaves. The windows
Flickered eyelids with oblique
Pupils of lamplight muffled beyond the glass.
Some houses were grandees. Others wore
Palm-fringes at their throats and seemed
Sorcerers whose dream-clouded eyes
Fluoresced like aggies. At the banyan's thunderous
Foot we gambled on mumblety-peg. I saw
Spiders blazing coldly like far-off stars
While the pink dewdrops wobbled on their webs.
An ancient scorpion dwelt behind the broom.
Its warm brown eyes gazed in two rows from the tip
Of its head like the curtained windows of a ship.
Its immobility made me dream of voyages.
And the blue-muscled skinks along the pebbles
Sported tuxedo-twills down their deceptive backs.
There I pierced a grasshopper with a sharpened match
And once, in a solution hole
Of the hammock, I bellied deep into the moist
Limestone crevice of a decaying reef. The earth
Smelled fresh as a new-worn shoe. I could have
Lain forever in that unmarked place. The soft
Desperate moths at nightfall sealed our house
Where all the thresholds were spelled. The brass
Hours chimed from the London clock and the moon
Trembled in white branches at the windowsill.

Live Oak, with Bromeliads

The live oak tufted with bromeliads
By the salt lagoon looks almost scarred.
Airplants bristle on its grey
Limbs like knotted sprigs of surgeon's thread.
In sprawling notches of the canopy
Spanish moss dangles in snarled clusters
While the long sunshine of Miami's winter
Lends it a gloss of fractured malachite.

But nothing could be less wounded than this oak.
Its knuckled roots infiltrate the dank
Marsh of the hammock, they drink the sand
Riddled by land-crabs to a moon-pocked surface.
And look:
              Like praying candles in a smoky shrine
Set up to honour the salt god of the marsh
The ranked branches embrace their parasites.

Fragrances

The threshold of your mother's room had such
Intimate possession of itself, and that
Satin fabric that the lamp assumed
Among the vanities, the combs and pins . . .
Complexities of being soft and cool,
Intricacy of clothing, lace and tulle,
The look of the half-shut chiffonier
With all the lank, loose-folded garments there;
The colours of her things in the dim lamp—
Almost unsayable, that gentian sleeve.

And sometimes I would hide in her wardrobe
Standing among the dresses and the gowns
As though a rush of women circled me
With a smell of warm and fragrant skin
Mingled with lilac and the blush of sun,
Just as the golden sunshade made a glow
In which we all looked suddenly transformed,
Illumined in the fragrance of the sun
That had a tinge of everlastingness,
The way verbena lingers on the tips
Of all your fingers when you say goodbye.

Florida Bay

A flittering of breeze, so hesitant,
Rustles my face before the sun is up,
So subtle that it seems the diffident
Touch of my children's fingers on my cheek.
I sit there with a wobbly coffee cup
Cocked on one drowsy knee. For over a week
This tender, pre-dawn breeze has signalled day.
It blows here from the south, from Florida Bay,

Where Florida curves westward to the Gulf,
The continent's dead-end, our Finistère.
If you turn inward now to find yourself
As you once were, you will ignore that breeze
With its humid scent of flowers. There,
In the brightening room old recollections tease
And elude you in forgotten things
While morning flickers with admonitory wings.

I used to wonder why I felt so out,
Not seeing that it was my mulish nature.
And now, at fifty, when I've just about
Finished with childhood (though dissatisfied),
The child's desolation, his nomenclature
Of loneliness, projected and identified
With the furniture of Sunday dining rooms
After the pot roast and the macaroons,

Still so possesses me.
                         And though we leave
The darkness of their tears behind the door,
Shut our ears to their cries, refuse to grieve
For those we hated with the force of love,
Their desperation not to be forgotten or
Forsaken follows us till we are victims of
Every laceration of their breath
That will not leave us even in their death.

And desolation will always be those warm
Miami afternoons when August rain
Accumulated in the distance, before the storm
Amassed and broke, and plump drops lashed
The tattered fronds outside, or hurricane
Roared from Tortugas north with stillness stashed
Inside its eye, and we waited for the wind
To flay the stucco and leave the banyan skinned.

Waiting, waiting—childhood solitude
Of toys in the moted morning sun—
O intimations of a requiem. The mood
Befell me like the sweet metallic tune
Of a Sunday carrousel before the ride is done,
That sense of perpetual and soon-
To-be-cherished happiness . . . Remember your surprise
At the candled mirrors that returned your eyes

In diamond encirclings till you'd spot
An icicle kaleidoscope of yourself
Amid the ponies' melodious trot,
And think, Is that me? Is that my face?
As though a stranger lent you a strange self
That stared back at you from the secret place
Mirrors rise out of, or the near-familiar look
Of photos of cousins tucked in an old school-book.

Remember the smell of the hall bookcase?
Inside the little mullioned panes that held
Embrittled paperbacks, you saw your face
Compromised by shadows and were scared,
While with a smudging fingerprint you spelled
The titles of the books in French or stared
At foxed engravings in the Illustrated
London News, its fashions of the celebrated

Looking so weird in the Miami light,
The roach-specks and the spider-silk impressed
With long-squashed rosebuds in a tome clapped tight
For decades. And dead cousin Arthur's photograph,

His First Communion suit, his parents dressed
In ascots and in flounces, a pleased faint laugh
Beginning at the corners of his mouth,
Among shrill memorabilia of the South:

Taffeta bows, a dance card, a leather purse
Embossed Havana, steamship souvenirs,
Pearl opera glasses, scraps of verse
In coffee-coloured copperplate, a lock of hair,
Child's hair, beribboned, and the quaint gold shears
That snipped it, in a reticule. Aware
Even then of the poisons of the past,
You touched these keepsakes warily at the last.

Is this where desolation began?
In that artifice of intimacy
I suffered then? I was the "little man,"
The fragile simulacrum of the male
Swaddled in fisticuffs and mock gentility.
I puffed a self out on the sail
Of my matchbox boat that skimmed the pond,
Its makeshift mainstay bowing as it swanned.

You'll know mementoes by their bandages,
Their plush and tissue gauzes: safe from life!
They are embowered like the unopened pages
In those old volumes you would puzzle over,
Their signatures uncut by the curious knife
And only dreamy fade-marks on the cover.
But in the end I'll pack the books away
And go outside, drive south, toward Florida Bay

Where the peninsula, above the Keys,
Opens into an unimpeded view.
There once I saw the white birds from their rookeries
Of bobbing islands clatter up and fly
And though I cling to memory, as if I knew
Devotion were fiercer than that wing-divided sky,
I'll bow before them as they skim the ground:
Outside ourselves is where our selves are found.

Highway Grasses

The subtle undulations of the grass
Along the highway held the shape of the wind.
The grassblades stooped like fragile flames
Of candles ruffled by a child's
Puffed breath, then seemed to cower down,
Enfolded their stalks with neighbour stalks
In a seethe of symmetry.

                             The roadside grasses
Tossed back while the wind defined itself
Against their festive tassels, and their unison
Moved me more than the delicate
Nugget colours of their swaying stems,
Or the breathing bunches of sound
Their tops together gave, like
Conversations carried by the wind
In a language you can hear but not
Make meaning of.

                             The pleasure of the tall
October grasses on the highway to the south
Rippled along their simultaneous
Stalks the way affectionate laughter
Moves the guests to lean across the table
Closer to each other, momentaneous
Communities.

Savannahs

Here the statues turn to fountains, here cascades
Commandeer the dreams of roustabouts, here
Smokestacks have a sheen of abnegation, and
The mortifying pleasures of the pool
Nuzzle our nerve-ends with their premonitions of
Some luminance of bodies, of the flesh
Made pure and whole beyond disdain, and we
Acknowledge the savannahs of our origins,
Those smooth, descending pastures to the sea,
As though the sea spelled freedom or as though
Its candour could awaken our dull eyes, as
Though its bitter liberation on the tips of our
Tongues announced some life resumed, some
Pearl-embedded possible, some promise still
Embowered, though only in the memories of words
Do the lashed waters yip and congregate,
And rain along the violet skin of the waves
Puckers like stings along a horse's hide.

I knew only the yearning of savannahs,
The delicate monotonies of grass-stems
Proffering some tasselled pagination of the wind,
And something of the exultation of
My knees, so long ago, the ecstatic
Scars of elbows, gave me back
The pebble-rainbows of the unloved ground.
There were no wings unequal to my heart then.
I sifted music through
The deft tendrils of my fingertips,
As though the heart were estuary to
That island-gathering, astringent sea.

Cellar

This is where we keep them: toy trucks
With busted wheels, the broken stuff
We can't get rid of, our old books,
The splintered chair, the fractured tabouret.

There's something stagey in our garbage.
The furniture is theatrical and grim.
Our repudiated gestures still live there,
Six feet under the kitchen. They wear
The vague insulted look of slighted relatives,
Belonging, but pushed aside.

                            The dark place gives
Reluctant nobility to these disowned things.
I picture other broken objects down here,
Not always on view: behind the dead palm,
A litter of stillborn phrases, the snapped
Bunches of words, the shivered promises,
Those dusty entreaties that still snatch the throat

—importunate as panhandlers or evangelists,
Those smirking beggars around Christmastime
Whose shrill clothes shine in the snowy light.

Mullein

"A pleasure secret and austere."
—Archibald Lampman, "In November"

"And mossy scabs of the wormfence, and heaped
stones, and elder and mullen and pokeweed."
—Walt Whitman, "Song of Myself"

1

Death is a kind of opportunity,
Deprivation possibility,
Where this weed strikes its root.
The mullein's infinitesimal black seeds
Crave for vacancy to germinate.
It startles me to see it colonnade
Defoliated roadsides and in June, impressed,
I round its plush and nettled obelisk.
From winter-clenched rosettes it pokes, man-high,
And grows big and green where other green things die.

All verticality, the mullein has a plumed
Columnar stature with up-curled
Leaves that stand out from its stalk
Like stiffened shavings on a whittled stick.
And from these curlicue-attentive leaves
The raceme of the mullein with
Its padded shaft ascends, a quilted
Polygon. And all along the raceme's
Naked length, little flowers appear,
Yellow-petalled to the pinnacle.

2

In vinyl bedrooms of cold-eyed hotels,
When I'm unable to imagine home

And when my own grim turn of mind
Depopulates familiarity
And nothing can people my sleep again,
I sometimes glimpse a mullein by the weed-
Whacked border of the parking lot,
Invisible though so conspicuous
Beyond the stuttering whiteness of the flood-
Lit asphalt, or poplaring a sewer-pipe,

And I like the way, from what nobody else
Would bother with, it sends a column up.
I like that it domesticates
Small desolations and that it pinches place
From peripheries where places cannot be
And that its wispy petal sweetens haggardness.
I like out of how little mullein makes
A shade. So it can mollify the bleak
Suite, the long hours of the night coming on,
That lurid doily with its Gideon.

3

If I were given to apostrophe,
I'd say to mullein, "Poke up, sprout, extend!
Be opportunistic, shrewd, exuberant.
Along storm gutters or the rims
Of gaudy troughs of algae-ruffled seepage,
Still be gauntly numerous, redeem the brink,
Sentinel the emptiness seraphically.
Drive your root in nihil till it spout
And flutter out, to pleasure flies and bees,
Your thin yellow flowers of astonishment.

Childhood House

For my brother Alan

After our mother died, her house, our
Childhood house, disclosed
All its deterioration to our eyes.
While living she had screened us from, or we hadn't seen,
The termite-nibbled floorboards and the rotting beams,
The wounded stucco hidden by shrubbery, the frayed
Unpredictable wiring and the clanking labour
Of the hot water line into the discoloured
Tub; the fixtures in the dining room
Skewed and malfunctioning.

                            I remember thinking with a
Swarm of confusion that this was the true state
Of our childhood now: this house of dilapidated girders
Eaten away at the base. Somehow I had assumed
That the past stood still, in perfected effigies of itself,
And that what we had once possessed remained our possession
Forever, and that at least the past, our past, our child-
Hood, waited, always available, at the touch of a nerve,
Did not deteriorate like the untended house of an
Aging mother, but stood in pristine perfection, as in
Our remembrance. I see that this isn't so, that
Memory decays like the rest, is unstable in its essence,
Flits, occludes, is variable, sidesteps, bleeds away, eludes
All recovery; worse, is not what it seemed once, alters
Unfairly, is not the intact garden we remember, but
Instead, speeds away from us backwards terrifically
Until when we pause to touch that sun-remembered
Wall, the stones are friable, crack and sift down,
And we could cry at the fierceness of that velocity
If our astonished eyes had time.

Old Photographs of Children

The cracked and spotted photographs
Of children dead a century before
Pierce us when we look at them.
The glister of an eye
Long consigned to cinders and
The maggot's mercies
Engages our gaze.

How near these children seem to us
And yet, how intimate with
Nothingness, as though for them
The double kingdom lay
Already open as a realm of light.
The sureties of hopefulness
Burning in their long-dead look
Disturb our uncertainty, refuse
Our knowledge of a future that awaits
Beyond the borders of the photograph.

We have the superior sense
That we encompass these children in their ignorance
Of all that happened since they left their pose,
Unless we come to see how they elude
All our displaced solicitude,
Their silver and palladium faces clasped
In the fragile grandeur of daguerrotypes.

Garter Snake

The stately ripple of the garter snake
In sinuous procession through the grass
Compelled my eye. It stopped and held its head
High above the lawn, and the delicate curve
Of its slender body formed a letter S—
For "serpent," I assume, as though
Diminutive majesty obliged embodiment.

The garter snake reminded me of those
Cartouches where the figure of a snake
Seems to suggest the presence of a god
Until, more flickering than any god,
The small snake gathered glidingly and slid,
But with such cadence to its rapt advance
That when it stopped once more to raise its head,
It was stiller than the stillest mineral
And when it moved again, it moved the way
A curl of water slips along a stone
Or like the ardent progress of a tear
Till, deeper still, it gave the rubbled grass
And the dull hollows where its ripple ran
Lithe scintillas of exuberance,
Moving the way a chance felicity
Silvers the whole attention of the mind.

Of Paradise as a Garden

For Ricardo Pau-Llosa

The symmetry of cycads with their fire-coloured
Cones and mandala-fringed fronds, the
Precarious peace of epiphytes, orchids
With long-suffering corollas, the whiteness
Of vanilla's petals and that scent . . . And
There are here small advantageous vistas
Where you glimpse across lagoons
The only infinities we're ready for—
That faded, hardly bluish edge of sky
With its reminiscent tint. Here the shade
Of colonnades affords
Presentiments of paradise, the lanes
Not of some featureless peace
But of calm among spontaneous
Freshets, exploratory orders that bemuse
The intellect, and a continual
Undisappointed hope, not as yearning but
Anticipation, not hope as torment,
As it is in life, but all the pleasures
Of fulfilment there, a longing that is
Ever realized, the loveliness of the familiar,
The alphabet of friendship learned again,
Not loneliness but only the garden's green
Where all the exiles find their homes again.

(Fairchild Gardens, Miami)

The Courtesy of Old Oblivion

"Mein Trost ist: Lethes Wasser haben
Noch jetzt verloren nicht die Macht,
Das dumme Menschenherz zu laben
Mit des Vergessens süsser Nacht."
—Heine, *Zum Lazarus*

The courtesy of old oblivion,
Its etiquette of kind forgetfulness,
Means Lethe is a liquor that we sip
In charcoal estimations of antiquity
Until the tongue in its papillae scrolls
A common genealogy of smoke.

Forgetfulness is like a gentleman
Who spreads his coat upon the nakedness
Of all the terror in the family tree.
Against amnesia he willingly
Proffers that tiny, antiquated taste
Of sweetened darkness for our approbation—

Soft-spoken, with his floppy collar loose,
And gentle eyelids with the shape of night.

Halifax

Everyone enfolds a city so
Cordoned from the ordinary, pinnacled
And musketed, with steeples
Sleek in their stickling rectitude;
Remote and rainy, on its point of sea,
With pomp of foghorns pulsing from the buoys.

Such inward cities have the radiant
Tedium of childhood. There
The salt-scathed asphalt shone and the prim
Crimson of the bandstand, in
The Public Gardens, echoed
November's roses. There the decorous
Chrysanthemums inaugurated
Avenues of rain.

These hidden cities have the homeliness
Of Haligonian Sundays in the fall,
After the service, when the reverend
Fumbled the sermon and the gawky choir
Still thumped and trilled so woefully,
And all the heaviness of afternoon
Poured down, until the emblematic
Windows of the saints
Bared their antimonies.
All life is heaviness
In secret cities when November comes.

In Halifax the shrill ferry already
Sloshes at the prompt piers. A seagull
On a scavenged bag
Mewls into the saturated sky.
The cities of remembrance all are ports
Where every Sabbath of the autumn tolls
And even weeping feels gratuitous.

The Public Gardens

The Public Gardens are so cunningly
Laid out. The boxwood has symmetrical
Barbarity of shape. And the walkway
With its fractal jaggedness dissuades
The eye. Linden colonnades will shine
Like faces at a solemn protocol
Brushed with tears. In November, the long line
Of the damp trees oppresses. The blades
Of the tall grasses spiral sinuously.
There is such a definitive edge to the border
Of the hoed-up beds. This is a place of order
Despite its delicate wilderness disarray.

Here, three years ago, I watched a swan
Trundle in a chicken-wire enclosure
Like something perishable stored up for the spring.
The swan looked muddy and obese.
Its horny, latex-coloured feet unnerved
Me. This was not the virile, ominous
Swan of Yeats, the gliding cynosure
Of all imagination. Only a close-docked wing
Remained of all that majesty. Beyond the wan,
Superannuated roses, brambled and brown-edged,
Full of some fear that I could taste, police
Cars by the black gates wetly reconnoitred
Where hunched unshaven men smoked and loitered,
And the festive statues, rain- and mildew-ledged,
Gestured spaciously with luminous
Fingers where the civic soot collected.

The swan brought back to mind a horrible
Thing I'd seen there once, a hungry seagull
Perched upon a half-dead mallard's back
And eating its raked and squirming flesh alive.
It might have been hideously symbolical—
The mystical amalgam of two beasts

In which the stronger on the weaker feasts—
But for the pitiful, writhing, bony neck
Of the injured duck. Its pain deflected
Darwinian pieties, too bland in any case to give
Individual significance to pain,
And I remembered how, some weeks before,
I'd eaten roast duck with a rich plum sauce.
Here was the flesh itself, with crass
Thrashings agonizing, while the quick gull tore
Slivers of slitted skin and dabbled its bill again
In flinching meat.

                   Pain estranges,
Cordons the sufferer and disarranges
Pity in its strict perimeters:
I thought of people I'd known, sufferers
So perimetered by pain that only love
Could touch them still—sometimes, not even love.

With a stick I chased away the gull above
And then I laid the stick along the torn duck's neck
And leaned until it broke with a little click
And both its wings fanned out reflexively,
Tremoring and hovering and an almost terrible
Exhilaration poured along my hands and arms,
Though I also felt the nausea you feel
When pain intrudes on beauty and disarms
The order obligatory for the beautiful,
And I knew how much I'd loathed that hurt bird
That had suffered so like me,
Or you, in muddy miserable twitches, wincingly.

I left the Public Gardens with its rows
Of neatly mattocked beds, I, a poet, one of those
Virtuosos of the nerves, and what had I seen,
Suppurative, shame-naked, and obscene?
In muted wards, some agony unwinds;
Beyond the still facades, behind Venetian blinds,
Some passion enacts its ritual

Desecration of the actual.
The horror in my mouth was almost prayer,
The stumbled syllables of those in despair,
And yet, so poetical, so apposite!
Does order merely gauze the infinite
Wince of the debrided skin? And was pity
Conferral of extinction or the first stone of the city
Founded in love?
That day, I saw the fountains with their casual
Music of refusal
Splash beyond while in its pen the great
Mud-spattered swan beaked its black gate.

Railway Stanzas

I have always found railway stations sad.
The aura of departure lingers there.
The rails that stretch away in parallel
Abraded brightnesses dismay, like those problems
In your old mathematics book at school;
Outmoded, they yet sting the intellect
With formalin conundrums of the time that's left.
I think of all the leavetakings I've known.
Airports are abstract. Railroads have
Valedictory fragrances—the seethe of steam,
A scorched whiff of oil. I think of
Lovers waving as the platform fades.

And yet, a hankering for depots, terminals,
Is a symptom of good health, a robust mind.
Arrivals also figure in my dreams
Where they take on the shape of engine spokes.
I used to see the spokes and wheel as a frieze,
Not as an engine but a dark geometry,
Tableaux of pistoned possibilities,
Without a single ledge for tears,
Without the ineluctable hankie of farewells,
The blurred mascara of a momma's eyes,
Dad's mustache all atremble, baby's howls,
The structure of forsakenness as the station speeds

Out of sight and hearing into memory:
The dainty Edwardian melancholy
Of junctions, switching-places, water tanks;
The bright red afterthought of the caboose
With men, suspendered, sucking corncob pipes
On the little black-railed platform at the back;
And there was also the sleek smell of rails,
The bitter cloudiness of iron gauge,
The creosote-soaked ties and the gouging spikes,
The deferential signal-bars, the throb of the shrill

Light. But most, a pale opacity of windows
In a nighttime train, a glimpse of shaded lamps

And diners all embraced in goldenness
And wisps of smoke, the porter leaning between
The sleeper and the observation car—
Watched in a shriek of speed from a trestle by
The slow, muddy river underneath.
And sometimes I had stuck a silver dime
To the outer rail before the train went by
And now retrieved it as the distance took
That companionable apocalypse away:
The coin was faceless now and hammered flat
And it felt hot and smooth and was transformed
In my fingers to a fossil of velocity.

I do not write this from nostalgia.
I who once revered as a mercy of
Certitude the benignity of fact
Am sceptical of every revery
That leads me backward into dubious time.
A sense of destination, though, beguiles
Me still, the piercing and metallic scent
Of almost indiscernible adieux.
It is momentum now that holds me, the
Quick kiss on the steps, the conductor's
Cry, the stirring of the great black wheels
In spires of steam toward their unyielding speed.

Grasses in November

In November the grasses discover
Fountains in themselves
That cluster upward toward the long stalks'
Tips and flourish cloudy flowers
That are the oblique colour of the sun.

They look festive, ceremonial, like
Ostrich feathers in a vestibule;
And yet, they seem so public, plumed
For display, and wag from side to side
In the cold breeze that nudges them
Prancingly like horsetails in a stately parade
Or shaggy pompoms brandished
To the booming of a drum.

Getting Ready for the Night

When Grandma combed her fine white hair at night
Until it toppled to her shoulderblades
In startling cascades, bright-angel-winged,
She looked like Milton's seraph at the gate
Of paradise: sovereign, ingenuous and stern.
I marvelled in the ripples of her hair
The teasing and impertinent lamplight touched.
But, "Won't you clip my toenails for me now?"
She said and then, with a stoic sigh,
"It's hard to be so old, so incapable."

I didn't want to touch her pallid foot
And yet, it felt astonishing when her left
Foot nestled in my clasp and I began
Scissoring the wrinkled horn of nail
With snipping shears until the pale
Translucencies of toenail ribboned off.
Her sole felt warm in my deft paw.
And suddenly I could appreciate
Grandma being mortal, one who sheds
Skin and nails and all integuments.

                    But then she twined
And spooled her colourless flat hair
About accustomed fingers into supple
Braids
              And I was baffled in the tenderness
Her silk-shaded light winked down on both of us.

                  I snipped her toenails
Evenly. Together we prepared her
For the night. Together we made sure
That shorn and braided, she would enter into
The encirclements of darkness just beyond
The pooled, penurious
Empire of the lamp.

Nova Scotia

"The topography is of slight relief, and innumerable
lakes, streams, bogs, barrens and stillwaters occur."
—*Flora of Nova Scotia* (1945)

For David Solway

Here, south of Halifax, near Peggy's Cove,
Where the coastline shoulders out into the sea,
You search the landscape for its difficult
Splendour. There are sudden gullies and domes
Littered with glacial boulders in a jagged
Equipoise. The glacier's nosing wedge
Dishevelled all the hillsides and the stones
Seem sprinkled by a child. Gargantuan
Spills of granite balance on dainty
Hillocks and the mauve arroyos
Have a stunned and smoky look
Like gaping survivors of some detonation.

Each thing seems hieroglyphic to your eye.
Tough decumbencies of spurge
Thicken the glance. The cheeks of rocks
Are bearded with lichens in rough,
Persistent whorls. Sometimes in a crevice
Of the castup rock you'll come upon
Improbable orchids or a bullfrog croaks
From one of the many little pools of rain
Skittered by windblown spray. Maybe you'll find
Fragments of shell and glass that have
The cadence of the North Atlantic in their
Sleek, barbaric shapes. But
The narrow pathway twists between
Contiguous desolations, indifferent
To history, and there is
The momentary, quickly avoided sense

That all we cling to here is scaffolding
Above slashed granite and the ocean's voice.

You won't sing hymns to seals
Along the sharp immersions of this coast
Nor will you drink transfiguring
Mouthfuls of the pure and bitter wind
From your chill chapped hands.
But maybe there your moment will arrive
Unaccompanied by memory
Or expectation and you'll see
Simply what lies before you or ahead,
Observe it with a purgatorial
Precision of the eye
And speak it in the justice of the tongue.

Later, beyond the coastline you will come
Out of season to the dark hotel
Where your room overlooks the sea.
The gaudy awnings will be rolled up for the spring,
The seaward patio swept bare, the hulls
Of summer's pleasure boats aligned
And tarpaulined, and maybe there will be
A single lantern with its oily light
Reflected in the ocean of November.
There in your seclusion from the wind
All night in dreams of home you'll listen for
The cold companionship of distant waves,
Hear squalls beating and the seethe of foam.
Abstracted from particulars, alone
With the uncertain fluttering of your breath,
You'll listen to rafters creaking and the clack of glass
And in the faroff vehemence of that darkness, still
Suspended between memory and hope,
All night you'll hear
The North Atlantic, just beyond the cove,
Banging its knuckles on the heartless sill.

III

FOR A MODEST GOD

For Irena

do stříbra jsem vyryl
SINE AMORE NIHIL
bez lásky není nic.

"In silver I have incised this verse
SINE AMORE NIHIL
without love is nothingness."

—Jan Skácel, *Sonet jako talisman*

Quark Fog

Let matter take on the shape of elands,
The hieratic pongo or the great
Eager emptiness in the spaces of love.
I ponder the temporary desert
Of my hand. Matter will not
Chisel a voice from this
Fog of quarks.

If merest fable drops into the fog,
Articulated stars assert
Eclosion of the gold-sewn chrysalids.
Early nouns bob in blunt fens.
Verbs browse electrically in mist.
Particles gnarl the stems of bulrush copulae.
In a pristine caldera of consonants,
Vowel-magma brims
And virginal horizons spike
Cordilleras of speech.

Sweetheart,
Let haggard worlds await
The proton's aboriginal decay:

Our sun is uttering her saffron palatals.

I

Ô ressources infinies de l'épaisseur des choses, rendues par les ressources infinies de l'épaisseur sémantique des mots!

—Francis Ponge

Gazing at Waves

At Morbihan or Montauk or at Peggy's
Cove, or where the little drab cornice
South of Casablanca runs to sand,
Wherever there's an ocean promontory,
People always look far out to sea
As though expecting some unheard-of
Apparition to arise, beyond the waves
Where the horizon glitters like an eye
Peeping through a sleepy eyelid.

                           Why
Do they look so searchingly out there?
Do they think the sea can offer more
Than corrugated combers or
That queasy smell of peaches that the shore
Concocts from mussel shells and clumps of kelp?

Maybe there's satisfaction in the prompt
Pinnacles of waves, their tasseling
Symmetrical ascensions, and that sense
Precision amid pandemonium
Provides.

At other times, more rarely now perhaps,
Some little shiver of acknowledgement
Still finds us there
Between the stately troughings and the
Counterglides, the scattered plash
Of droplets, with the keen gulls
Mewing and the rocks
Reflective of a light too old for us,
And this gives back our
Littleness again, this restores
Some sort of privileged insignificance;
Or will the waves always appear mere
Sequent arrival without consequence?

The spectacle is sovereign, yet intimate.
How soon the waters enter our
Attention, follow us in sleep,
Accompany the cadence of our minds,
Seem punctual and seriatim, curled
In all the beauty of futility,
So promptly mortal as they gather in,
Ascend and hover in the gusting air,
Then amble over into hiddenness,
Fold themselves in sand like drowsy claws
Curved into the twilight of the nest.
Is it a consolation to be witnesses
Of what so lucidly evades our gaze?
Is gazing a favour that gazed waves bestow?

What It Is Like To Be A Bat

Night is algorithmic; dark,
Archimedean. Cosines of echo
Structure the night. A peep
Subtends from the slick
Bodies of crickets. The gauzy
Reverberations of moths are not
The curt returns from smokestack or from arch.

Night is a cloth, crinkling
With secret threads, alert
To the listening ear as any sun.
Night is a calculus
Of cries where bodies are
Connected in the parallax
Of coincident voices, ripple-precise.

Night plinks with voices.
There are the torn orbits
Of escaping voices, the stridulence
Of beetles, steely timbres of the katydid.
There are loving collocations
Of ridges known only by sound-shadows, loud
Shards of home demarcated by pipings
In darkness beyond all superfluities
Of sight. There are the welcoming crests
Of other cries, sweeter than the green
Panic of lacewings, that phosphor
All along the sleep-furred, down-
Gloved bodies of our caverned families.

The Ant Lion

Beneath your shoe soles there's a beautiful
Concavity of sand, a symmetrical
Funnel the width of a small boy's thumb.
It looks expertly smooth. Precarious
Sand grains have been set to slide
Whenever a plodding ant's insouciance
Pitches it down that soft declivity.
The owner of the pit abides down there,
A drab predator the colour of
Quarry rock, old spackle, gypsum, slate.
Earth-coloured, with the shadows of the earth,
He snuggles in the hollow of his snare.

At night, in childhood, I would sometimes dream
Of the panicky scrambles of a slipping ant,
Its scurrying despair that swept it down
Irresistibly along the volatile sand.
The way that dreams deceive you the ant fell
And I, asleep, felt falling too
Through filmy floorboards into avalanche
As the heart-stopped terror of my helpless dream
Tossed me to the steep mouth of the pit.

There, with upswung jaws, the ant lion
Wiggled out of ambush, rushed to hug
Me, his frantic victim, in a pinch. That
Too had the horrible embrace of dream
Where you choke those you love or they choke you
And everything takes place mechanically
Despite the shrieked beseeching of your will.

After the waving prey is tugged below
To be consumed in secret, beneath the dirt,
The ant lion's slow return looks dreamlike too.
There's a proprietary fussiness,
Meticulous, almost suburban, as
The little killer scrapes his whirlpool smooth.

An Oak Skinned by Lightning

The oak tree skinned by lightning is ringed round
With wood-lice trails on its inmost bark.
The scars of the oak startle: each mark
Of its once-hid flesh revels in profound

Asymmetry our eyes must dote upon.
The random meanders of the blind wood lice
Cut their labyrinthine cicatrice
Of cryptic squiggles in soft cambium.

Their carved grooves look like staves and notes of scores
A cello ellipsoidally transmutes
Before the main theme flutters to the flutes.
I feel these clear canals. My fingers parse

These worm trails laid bare like epigraphy.
The oak was Christlike as the lightning stripped
Its seamless raiment off and the rain whipped
It while it shook, a suffering being, in July

When even dragonfly and hawkmoth seem benign.
I am moved by the incommunicable script
Of the lightning on the oak tree's swept
Pith. Is this the idiolect of summer, the sign

Our eyes are aching to decode,
These edicts from a cancelled chancery,
These mute communicados of the sensory,
Whose each jot seems a letter in a word?

My fingertips Champollion the oak;
The burined lice trails teach my skin.
Here hands alone, not eyes, draw you within
The secretive syllables the lightning struck.

Rooster

For Tippy

I like the way the rooster lifts his feet,
So jauntily exact,
Then droops one springy yellow claw aloft
Just like a tailor gathering up a pleat.
And then there are those small surprising lilts,
Both rollicking and staid,
That grace his bishop's gait,
Like a waltzer on a pair of supple stilts
Or a Russian on parade.

I like the way he swivels and then slants
His red, demented eye
To tipsy calibrations of his comb
And ogles the barnyard with a shopkeeper's stance.
Sometimes his glossy wattles shudder and bulge
As he bends his feathered ear
And listens, fixed in trance.
When drowsy grubs below the ground indulge
And then stretch up for air,

How promptly he administers his peck,
Brisk and executive,
And the careless victim flipflops in his grip!
I like the way his stubby little beak
Produces that dark, corroded croak
Like a grudging nail tugged out of stubborn wood:
No "cock-a-doodle-doo" but *awk-a-awk*!
He yawps whenever he's in the mood
And the thirst and clutch of life are in his squawk.

Chiefly I love the delicate attention
Of the waking light that falls
Along his shimmery wings and bubbling plumes
As though light pleasured in tangerine and gentian

Or sported like some splashy kid with paints.
But Rooster forms his own cortège, gowns
Himself in marigold and shadow, flaunts
His scintillant, prismatic tints—
The poorest glory of a country town.

A Crow at Morning

He paces toward our trash pile with a squire's
Proprietary stride. Wariness has stropped
His feathers' gloss. He is aubergine
Sleekness incarnate. His opulence
Stands mittened in a sooty radiance.
O raucous combustion,
Uncontained by your own black vanes!
You dignify my morning
With a coal chiaroscuro.
Your flat and avid eye
Now gloms some nugget and you plane
Your head with an optician's
Click-stop precision, a
Strangely childish
Flourish
Of your Benthamite
Beak which brute utility has honed
To its unerring edge. You
Lance a bag of ordure, you
Dance in, filch and shuddertuft
Your head, all
Snug yarmulke above your Hasid's
Melodious eye.

                    Even so,
Your feet (which swag the corners of my eyes)
Are pagan feet, nude
To the toes, abutting in bare claws.
Everything is *hefker* to your eyes,
And yet, lascivious indigo belies
The Mishnah of your gabardine.

Flamingos

1

My quarrel with your quorum, Monsignor
Flamingo, is that you scant the rubicund
In favour of a fatal petal
Tint. I would rather bask
In riots of the roseate
Than measure your footfalls'
Holy protocols beside the head-
Board of a drowsy demiurge.
I think God snores in rose
Leaves of serenity, not in your
Clatter of cadaverous vermeils.

2

I find flamingos beautiful Tartuffes
Who entice as they distance me.
When they display their billiarding
Adolescent sprawl of knees I
Remember the parochial
School girls in pink cashmeres, their rosy
Kneecaps polished by novenas.

3

Flamingos have the silhouettes
Of parking meters. They have no epaulettes
And yet seem always in uniform—
Little, stilted caudillos! They swarm
In unruffled ripples of defiling pink.
They mimic ballerinas and yet stink.
Flamingos are dirty in their purity,
Blazon Venezuelas of lewd suavity.
Beneath their transcendent, back-bent

Legs flamingos are somnolent
And lubricious birds whose stiff tutus
Amuse
The spoonbills and anhingas who erect
Nests of fish skin to reflect
The imperial smut of the sky.

                               I feel a samba roll
Under my eyelids when flamingos stroll
Oceanward at sundown and clap their stubs of wings
In gawky, rank, hierophantic posturings.

4

When the Lord God created the flamingos, He
Fell into despondency. He knew
That roseate feathers on such skeletons
Elicit incredulity. He gloomed
For days, obsessive as a poet who
Discovers a covert love affair between
Obstreperous syllables and then,
Cracking grandeur from the egg of shame,
Sets these
Diametric desperadoes in a pas de deux.

5

Only in Miami is supreme
Loneliness apparent in flamingo dawn.
The squalor of the place is cruelly pink.
There are pink curtains on the lousy shacks.
The impulse to adorn deepens the nakedness.
There flamingos all the color of a bone
Scavenge in vermilion stateliness.
Their pink flocks forage in that loneliness.

Anhinga

There is a callisthenic finesse to the neck
As the poke-stick of the beak
Comes up. The neck's loop revolves,
Too sinuous to be plausible.
This neck has innuendoes of a fish,
Must writhe and must wriggle and
Must pivot in sopping
Twists, distinctively drip-dry,
Till the rough feathers regain their brackish glare.

Eel-spasms, annular
Cascades, clamber the bayberry
Over the frilled sludge where the gar
Gelatinizes in its own repose.
The anhingas ogle the gorgeous sky
Over Shark River and as they gaze
Extend vespertilian
Wings, meticulous and moist.
They hold their pose.
It's almost reverential for those,
Like me, with worshipful proclivities
When these black birds spread out such wings.

O anhingas on the floodgates and the levee bridge,
You pray with nothing but water and I see
Your signatory darkness cloak the sun.

Turtle's Skull

The shore rang under my heel
After the squall: delicate eyelids
Of shell, the scattered audacities
Limestone confects: those peach-stung
Volutes of supersession, cowrie
And turkey wing, the murex with its
Acrid spirals and the bony rose
Of the lion's paw. Vacancies, all
Vivid! Where conch gongs trumpeted
Afternoons of disenchantment,
Poinciana-hosannas of departure,

I set the bare-scoured skull
Of the loggerhead seaward
And at daybreak, when the iron
Ladle of the eastern sky oozed its
Apricot-bold fissures of day,
Scathing water poured
From the eyes of the skull.
Black sockets wept the sea.

Coastlines

1

Barnacles cinch
Sea-battered pilings.
Dog whelks maraud in mud.
How the North Atlantic
Wrangles the rocks!
Above, the houses of the fishermen
Look matchstick but are fierce.
They hold to the skittish boulders with all their might.
Next door, in the wired-off
Graveyard of the cove,
The headstones lean aslant,
Scripture pages thumbed down by the wind.
Below them the ocean
Seethes and scathes all day,
All night, and the spray
Smokes where it slaps the shore.
Tide pools boil with foam.

On coastlines you realize
What world will last.
See how the lean light
Glances against granite.
Erosion gorges the coastline out,
Nibbles the gaps.
You feel a shiver in
The ocean's memory.

2

What if this coastal road, these roofs
Vivid against the ocean, these
Steeples and these gas
Stations, what if these docks and piers and
Marinas, these tough

White houses with their windowboxes,
Stood only in the minute's multitude?
What if each minute made its universe?
What if in our hands we held our world
Breakable and rainbow-velveted as mere
Wobbling bubbles that our children blow?
I feel my skin, I feel my face,
Yield to the light as coastlines yield,
Accepting the loving
Phosphorence of daylight's
Demarcation. I feel
The violence of all its delicacy.

3

Coastlines are where our opposites ignite
And no one can say, *After all, it's all right.*
Coastlines are where your father and your mother
Turn without a word forever from each other.
Coastlines are where the quick-footed sun
Touches Ultima Thule and can no longer run.
Coastlines are where we learn the ocean's tragedy:
Incessant endeavour, incessant panoply,
Broken down to crumbs of nothingness
And yet we want to bless
Each ragged repetition of the waves—

So inconsolable, so close to us.

II

The horsemen and the night and the desert know me,
And the sword and the lance, the paper and the pen.

—Abu Tayyib al-Mutanabbi

Mutanabbi in Exile

In alien courts I melodied for bread
But now the sordid business of verse
Enjoins me to this dry northern
Kingdom where disaffected ostriches
Snort at sundown and the prince
Idles the hours away with paradigms
In ancient grammar books.

A shabby gentility obscured my youth.
Poverty was a stench I couldn't scrub
And largesse smarted out of others' hands.
But language was immeasurable as shame
And burned in the beatific mouth of God—
He is exalted!—and now language flows
From my fingertips and from my quill
The way the spider tessellates its silk.

My heart is fringed with arrows like the sun
Or the chastened, wincing surface of a blade
Hammered in Damascus out of Indian steel.
My heart is like the chilly ramparts of cranes
Longing southward as the winter dawns.
But my lines still rustle lovely as the slide
Of rosaries of olive wood blessed by pilgrimage
Or the pages, startled as acacia,
In the whispering codices of the Law.

The moon enacts its faded casuistries
And there are thorn trees twisted like beggars
By the last stones of encampments, the dry
Dung of pack animals, and *thumam* grass
Stuffed in the fire crevices. There I stopped
And all my pain swept over me
In that smooth-blown place.
How could such meager anonymous shreds
Summon remembrance in a spill of tears?

South of Aleppo, where the stony mesas gust
With desolation and the jackal bitch whimpers
And snuffles in an unloved earth, my longing
Rang as hungry as the crows of winter.
The inkwell knows me, and the carven quill,
And the tense and crackling surfaces of parchment,
And swords and lances know me, and the strong horses,
And the night will remember me, and all empty places.

Mutanabbi Praises the Prince

The luscious reddening gold of the emir's coin
Buys my encomia. I haggle in magnificence
Or then I elbow-dust his aureole.
But such praise costs. The syllables are pearl
Nipped from the darkness of Bahrayni seas
By clever divers, or rubies of Kashmir
Pried from reluctant mines.

Let others gown the prince in obsequious fabrics
Or snuggle bracelets and rings of hammered gold
Over his wrists and fingers, or incense his hair
With myrrh or labdanum, or dunk his feet
In subtle unguents brought from Hadhramaut.
I garment him in the golden fragrance of praise
That gives men life forever, that will ring
In the shadowy mouths of the unborn,
His great-grandchildren's unimagined progeny,
In chains of consequence effected by the will
Of the Compassionate across ungenerated time.

Mutanabbi Remembers his Father

Sometimes, half in sleep, when the dreaming mind
Confuses past and present smokily,
So that dead friends and benefactors turn
And break into smile or greet you, unaware
That everything has changed forever now,
Or the unmistakable pressure of a hand
Consoles the shoulder of the child you were,
Sometimes, then, at such half-realized
Encounters, I can picture him again.
The past is knotted like the hempen length
That slides into the midnight of the well.
Each instant survives in darkness lost to us,
Perhaps cherished in the mind of the Merciful
The way remembering fingers cherish heirloom pearls.

I picture a man who lurches, like a crab,
Up stony alleys, who shudders like a pack mule
Under punishing burdens, who sets one wary shoe
Before the other as he stumbles and labors along.
Two tipping leather pails bounce on a pole
Slung across his arching shoulder blades—
A water carrier, a menial, bent and thonged
To his limber crossbeam, arching like a bow
And he the dark and devastating shaft
Ready to fly; or his cramped neck and arms
Seem lifted like the hawk's before he stoops.

This man is lashed
To the shame that glitters in his leather buckets
And he squawls all day in his haggler's croak,
"Waw-ter! Pure waw-ter!" A dented cup
Bangs at his breastbone. He is himself all
Thirst, the parched epitome of the sandy stretch
Between Kufa and Samawa, where I parsed my tongue
On redolent paradigms and measured the prosody
Of the subtle breezes that fluttered the tent flaps:

Mutafa'ilun, mutafa'ilun, fa'ilatun!—
The way grammarians vivisect a verse—
Or I lazed to the plangent amber of the oud.

That menial, that lugger of scummy drinks,
His eyes the sooty pink of a slaughter camel's lids,
His mouth cracked and cleft like a winter wadi,
His hands the paws of a Byzantine dancing bear—
That lowest of the low was my papa,
Water hauler for the swells of Kinda,
Who peddled the stuff of life so I could live
Like a prince of Hira in my gem-sewn silks
Among the purity of desert tribes whose speech
Glittered with the ancient rose-quartz clarity of Adam's tongue.

The Caliph

The wily and flamboyant Fatimid,
The intricate Caligula of God,
The neurasthenic delegate of prophets (may
God pray for them!), forbade all women
To wear shoes. He barred the cobblers from
Tapping their lasts or battering their little anvils;
Only poor prosodists could mime their hammer taps.

This, before he vaporized in the mauve
And umber desert of the air: al-Hakim,
Defender of the devious
Ambiguity of the Godhead, His penchant for
Bagatelles, creator of the paradox
Of sharks and swans, Draconian Comedian!

He placed an interdict on
Lamentation. He forbade women to
Weep at funerals, rescinded ululations,
And so each black cortège
Wound through the lanes of Cairo voicelessly.
Even sorrow is too great a liberty
Since it inhabits memory, citadel
Beyond the fists of despots, or of God.

And sometimes, in the pitch-light of the bazaar,
God's shadow baited bears or egged men on
To braggadocio or fisticuffs, or spied upon
Their most secretive gestures, their least
Askance innuendoes, their cupped whisperings;
Till, surrogate, he evanesced on the Muqattam Hills
One evening, leaving only slivered veils behind.

Perhaps only the forbidden know
The unshod deprivations of the dead,
And perhaps only children who've just learned to walk
Savor the nakedness of heels and soles.
Perhaps only the mad
Value the little freedom of the shoes.

III

"Was ist fröhlicher als der Glaube an einen Hausgott!"

—Franz Kafka, *Oktavheft 3*

Origins

I wanted to go down to where the roots begin,
To find words nested in their almond skin,
The seed-curls of their birth, their sprigs of origin.

At night the dead set words upon my tongue,
Drew back their coverings, laid bare the long
Sheaths of their roots where the earth still clung.

I wanted to draw their words from the mouths of the dead,
I wanted to strip the coins from their heavy eyes,
I wanted the rosy breath to gladden their skins.

All night the dead remembered their origins,
All night they nested in the curve of my eyes,
And I tasted the savor of their seed-bed.

Gravediggers' April

In winter we comfort our dead with talk.
We entertain them with our idle gossip.
We whisper the news while our breath freezes.
We line up at the storage shed where their bodies lie
Awaiting the great thaws of uncertain spring.
We tell them how the frost was dark this year
And steep, how business perked up at the quarries,
What happened to those botanists after the avalanche . . .

The padlock on their door is lumpy
With a blackened ice
But our damp spurts of breath revive
The grieving hinges. Murmurous petals of frost
Cloud the numbed metal.
                              And quicker now,
More hurried, as the whisperers file
Behind the convenience store:

It's comforting to chat even if
No answers return. The winter shapes our words.
The widower drinks, the widow squeezes shut
Her eyes, imagining the bluish stain
Corruption spreads across a loved complexion.
Come back! they whisper, *I'm lonesome here without you!*
But then, as the winter drags, *I'm glad you're there*
At last . . . where I can love you finally . . .

Beyond the door they lie
Snug in their salt till spring. Some prefer
The new crematory in Schenectady but for most
Of us winter is unthinkable without
The long peace of our conversations.

In April, when the gravediggers return,
Staggering, soused to the gills, on overtime,
And the black lock thaws into rusty rain

And they bear them out through the open shed
Into the flowering cemetery,

Then we can mourn.

Hand-Painted China

The slender cake plates had such fiery rims.
They caught the lazy radiance
Of afternoons like torch-
Light from a tomb. The old
Roses opened to my eyes
Their bold, embellished centers
Where a soft darkness had
Been stippled in. They drew down
My gaze until I felt
Labyrinthed in sweetness like a bee.

My great-aunts painted these.
The hesitant brush strokes on their
Undersides read "1893."
The greenness of their china does not fade
But witnesses an opulence the more forlorn
For being without issue. The pinks
And gilts, the raveled petals
Blowsy with magenta, importune
The fingers to partake of them.

These were the gravy boats of plenteous
Expectation, the creamers rich with dream;
These were the banquet platters, these
The hard yet fragile saucers, of trousseaux.
These were the festive dishes no one used.
Now they snag the curious
Light of afternoons
In magisterial shadow
Like a pharaoh's mouth.

                   Here,
In the lovingly abrasive, gently gritted
Impasto of hand-painted surfaces
That resist, like skin, with almost plush aplomb,
I feel some embodiment of all
Their expectations had the right to claim.
I feel their tentative fingertips touch mine.

Spider Silk

Once, when I gashed my finger, Grandmother
Led me to the closet down the hall.
There towels and bedsheets lay in fragrant folds
And an old, outgrown doll with bright-blink eyes
That scared me stiff with its hilarity
Drooled sawdust from its mouth onto a shelf.

Grandma pulled me close to her until
I understood the comfort of her touch.
She poked her free hand in the crevices
And spooled a spiderweb around her nails.
She wound the web again around my wound.
She daubed it tenderly until the clots of silk
Touched my blood and then my bleeding stopped
Almost at once.

                    There, among the smell of sheets,
In the cold, fresh, dark place that had scared me so,
Grandmother gave me her most secret smile.
Since that day,
Learning to love the doubleness of things,
I think the spider silk is in my blood.

The Suitors of my Grandmother's Youth

At dusk on Sabbath afternoons the slow-
Voiced suitors came, with awkward hat brims in
Their field-burred hands. They tipped themselves
On the very brinks of the Sunday chairs.
Their napes were fiery under their collar starch.
The knees of their blue serge suits looked rubbed and smooth.

Fireflies would be winking then, across the lawns.
Under the hedge, like small and sleepy stars
Witnessed through mist, they glittered and went out.
And everywhere, lilac would spire in June
Its chaste and promissory fragrance. Her
Sisters broke off sprays and clasped them
With half-ironic passion to their throats.
The boys were mute, traded long-suffering
Conspiratorial looks. On speechless
Strolls their beaux would hand to them
Desperate fistfuls of wild violets.
All their futures still appeared
Benign with promise, all their loves
Still hovered before the transactions of the blood.

The Gossip of the Fire

When Grandfather told us stories we
Bunched up close until our shoulders touched
Before the fireplace and as near the fire
As respect for its irascible
Outbursts would allow. Grandfather's words
Kept time with the fire that snapped
In the grate. Firecrackers of sap
Punctuated his thoughtful pauses.
The rhythm of the fire was intimate
And drew the whole world in. Outdoors,
Beyond the gossip of the fire, he said,
The creatures of the field stood listening,
Drawing some pensive pleasure from
The crafty coincidence of voice and blaze.
As Grandfather told his story we
Pictured the animals, beyond the bright,
Breathing beside us as our shoulders touched.

He spoke and a bullfrog's amber
Eyeballs held the moon. A red fox
With his curt, alacritous ears
Alert
Was savoring some specially resinous phrase.
The hens in their cozy ammoniac coop
Felt eggs emerging as his words emerged.

The creatures of the field, like us,
Were witnesses,
Attentive and yet vulnerable as those
Who witnessed without voice at Calvary,

And their eyes were radiant with anecdote.

Finding a Portrait of the Rugby Colonists, my Ancestors among them

It is as if you held them all, as God
Must have held them when He made their
Mouths, their shoulders, their irreplaceable
Eyes. It is as if their world were in your hands,
Here, in this rectangular beechwood frame
With the brown paper backing that complains like flame
With crackling annoyance when you tug the wire,
Bright-twisted, that sustained it on some wall.
There is a Godlike feeling to encompass so
On a flat, embrittled print their many lives,
Though only in effacement can you hope
To sustain their least regard.

To enter this
Beech-embrasured instant when a lens
With curatorial dispassion caught
Their momentary countenances asks
The modesty of trustful ignorance.
And though you cannot know them, yet you feel
Bone-closeness to their lives.

Tell me, if you had been
The God who shaped their cheekbones
And their brows, the dignified alertness
Of their ears, their ceremonial and
Formal smiles, their throats the patience of a
May sun mottled with its little dabs of luminance,
The fingers curved on Bibles or on canes,
The feet in their black-thonged propriety
Of dainty boots or strenuous clodhoppers,
Would you, for a world,
Have let them tumble into
Nothingness and seen their strong hearts rot,
Or would you have raised them up again,
The way you rouse a sleeper or a child?

For a Modest God

For Karin Solway

That fresh towels invigorate our cheeks,
That spoons tingle in allotted spots,
That forks melodeon the guested air,
That knives prove benign to fingertips,
That our kitchen have the sweet rasp of harmonicas,
That stately sloshings cadence the dishwasher,
That lobsters be reprieved in all the tanks
And mushrooms fetched from caverns to the light
And that the oil of gladness glisten down
The chins of matriarchs, anoint the crib;
That there be aprons of capacious cloth
Enveloping the laps of nimble chefs,
That our sauces thicken on the days of fast,
That the hearth cat frisk his whiskers and attend,
That no domestic terror smite our minds,
That midnights be benignant with a god's
Oven mitts and spatulas and solace-broths:

A little god, a little modest god,
A godkin in a shriven cupboard, Lares-
Palmable and orderly, presiding
Over the hierarchies of the silverware,
Our platters' strata and our serving spoons;
A small mild god, ignorant of thunder,
Attuned to nothing somberer than the trills
When all our crockery trembles to the fault
Of obscure, dimly rumorous calamities.

Rain in Childhood

On schooldays, when the windows of the bus
Dimmed with all our breath, we pressed up close
In jostling slickers, knowing the pleasure of
Being a body with other bodies, we children
A flotilla of little ducks, paddling together
On the wet ride to the schoolhouse door.
Once there, now toweled and dry, we looked outside,
Back where the hot, vociferous rain still fell
And stooped the trees and swung the traffic light
And pocked the yellow crosswalks till they fizzed
With all their gritty currents to the curb.

That steamy tar-damp smell of morning rain,
Its secret smokiness upon our mouths,
Surprised us with some sorrow of nostalgia.
Our past already had such distances!
Already in that fragrance we could taste
The end of childhood, where remembrance stands.

And when thunder pummeled the impending clouds—
Concussive ricochets that made the teacher
Hover with the chalk held in her hand—
We saw the lightning lace the school's façade
With instantaneous traceries and hairline fires,
Like a road map glimpsed by flashlight in a car.

IV

Blut ist ein ganz besondrer Saft.

—GOETHE, *Faust* I, line 1740

Baudelaire to Mme. Aupick at Honfleur (1867)

Chère Madame, do you remember still
The windows to the garden where we sat
Watching the sun on August afternoons
Lovingly ascend the leafy wall
As though it touched with radiance
Each object in its path: the tall
Stems of dahlias, the trellises
Where coiled brambles of young roses hung,
The statue of a nymph with hollow shell
Splashing the glittered water toward a pool
Where indolent carp swam in shadowy calm
Until the sun's long declination shone
Along the ripples that their bright fins caused?
Our conversations had the harmony
Of that ascending light. A tacit
Concord spoke from simple things.

When I remember those long afternoons,
The way the sunlight gently touched your hair,
Its infinitely tender kiss
Upon your lips and cheeks and eyelashes,
It seems to me our conversations were
Accompanied by light, were luminous,
And every word we spoke
Assumed serene embodiment in all
The voiceless objects that around us stood—
The linen with its darkly sparkling
Folds, the heavy lustre of the silverware,
The dense roses in their crystal mirroring
The calm crimson of the setting sun.

If I imagine Eden or a paradise
Where passion steeps its secret harmonies,
My memory is of those soft afternoons
When without speaking, or the need to speak,
The two of us admired the fading light.

Those were the last times that we had of such
Order made passionate in lucidity,
Of passionate innocence, passionate peace,
A love not governed by the torturers.

Salle des Martyrs

You see where blessed Théophane was nailed
To a ceremonial plank in mockery
Of the crucifix he brought benighted souls
And how expertly the Mandarin's men sawed
His anointed limbs, one by one, away. It is
The love, in these depictions of
His mutilations, which most horrifies.
Wherever mere agony fails to persuade,
Some clumsy, well-meant brush stroke puddles
The dipped blood. His silken slippers
Discolour in the reliquary
Darkness of the Martyrs' Room, among
Pyx, monstrance, and ciborium, the
Golden home of the shriek.
He wrote, "Only the weak
Are winnowed out for martyrdom."

We stare at his stark remains under glass—
His thongs and worm-riddled breviary,
His rosary with all its silvery
Decades yet intact. And here, in a nearby
Case beneath the gravelly loudspeaker, we
May find the instruments we used to use
On one another: the rust-serrated words,
The garotte of indifference, the swords
Of our separate nights, the grudging thumb-
Screws of speechlessness, and that so slow
Obliviating boot that grinds out love.

No tableaux will commemorate our loss,
No delicate daubs of calligraphy our crown.
The pre-recorded messages wind down.
Beyond the blood-freckled alb and chasuble
An eighteenth-century Christ, all ivory,
Fissures upon His cross.
And outside, in the moist Parisian noon,
The rosebushes draw their redness from this room.

Blood

For Dan and Chuck

1

All night in your ears you'll hear the blood sing
I am king!   I am king!   I am king!

You'll hear the ganged hammers of the blood erect
Its palaces. You'll feel the sluices of the blood connect

Its empires. Blood with its royal, rotten scent,
In its rush-lit vestments, in its vehement

Arabesques, dangles its scarlet manacles
Or glows like radium inside sly ventricles.

In stables where no savior lays his head
Blood shows its Balkan, its Rwandan, red.

Blood is apodictic in its contradictions,
Cascades from Adam's heart the crimson fictions

Of tribes and clans and families;
Knots the sinews with hot pieties.

2

Children not of my blood but of my love,
Whose sweet sonship is compounded of

All that mutual breath could make of hours,
We have plaited together what is ours

Minute by minute. Consanguinity
Knows nothing of our fierce fragility.

Blood relies
Hysterically on old school ties

While our enlacements all have been made
Thread by thread, braid upon braid.

3

When lawyers with their starry
Writs and decrees of certiorari

Banter your nativity,
Haggling some clotted pedigree,

Say, Blood should be slow, be slow,
Sound chuckle-melodic in heart's bungalow,

Be the hearthstone brightened by rich hemagogues,
The murmurous marrow of soft synagogues.

Let the vessels' cantillations in your throat
Dulcimer the temples' pulsing note.

For necklaces of ancestors twine love knots of time.
Backward to Eden let our recognitions rhyme.

Hate

Hate is so bracing and accommodates
Insight cozily. Hate icicles
The eyes. A happy hate rejuvenates,
Gladdens hair, pinks the cheeks, bicycles
Nimbly with the gusto of unchagrined exuberance.
An heirloom hatred's fun as well, accretes
In limestone ziggurats of bane. Hate lets you dance
On your own bones at last, and hate secretes

Warm poisons, lovely but so lonely
Venoms that pretext a hidden wish.
Obverse snugness of hate is only
Like love in that it's not squeamish
At all; grasps in a rush, with sleek grace:
To mangle—or to caress—the other's face.

Amber

For Irena

Prismed by amber, the insect's wing
Curves outward in a resinous nonchalance.
Casual fatality has paused in its dance.
I am tenderest when I touch this glozened thing.

Time's imagination stumbles me,
The way time tastes the roof beam's future ruin
Or calibrates the hovering, faint tune
In the siskin's wingbeat, with its brief veracity.

The stillness of surviving objects pleases
Our reveries. The inarticulate
Obduracy of a tigrine chip of agate
Spilled from a misplaced cuff link seizes

Our attention, so mere things appear
Stationary, resistant, and impervious.
The opera glasses, pearl-lensed, that will outlive us
Accord a terrible pleasure of mortality. We're

Cruelly honoured in our transience,
Evanescent instances of some unique
Reticulation. I hear you speak
Close to my ear. I feel your diffidence

As you slip your clothes and then your jewelry
And press against me till our nakedness
Warms us with momentous gentleness
And we lie hidden in that clarity.

History

This is our history.
The place is empty now where we began.
The rooms are full of sunlight, and the sea
Effaces all the traces where we ran.

I dreamt about the world before I was,
That darkened curve of shore, the stark
Clarity of coral undersea. Does
Broken coastline demarcate the dark

Of unbeginning daylight? Now I see
The twining light with all the dark I can.
This is our history:
The place is empty now where we began.

IV

ARABY

For David Solway

"Who has not loved the world from of old?
And yet, there is no way to be one with it."

—ABU TAYYIB AL-MUTANABBI

Jaham's Poetic Manifesto

"To make the ear
of the *khinzîr*
(that grotty pig!)
lustrous
as the Pleiades . . ."

Jaham pondered this and said:
Rather, to make the ears
of the Pleiades
pig-like, that is, porous, gristle-
webbed, conical, tendril-

attuned to the earth.

The Father of Clouds

Jaham in the Autumn Rains

The Father of Clouds sat surrounded by coffee beans
and the odor of roasting coffee filled the room.
When the beans had been ground and steeped
he poured the coffee the color of fresh blood
into the *baharjîyah* and the spice-pot fumed.
Scent of cardamom wheedled the hard-edged air.

In November, he said, God's angel herds the clouds
and drives them forward with a whistling stick.
Then, he said, the Sisters rule the night
and the fattening rains begin.

In autumn, when the signs of rain appear,
I can compose my verse. I drive the syllables
before me, I call *hâb hâb* to the clouds
of my words, I gather them in tumultuous
corrals. The colts of my sinuous vowels
tug against the leather of my consonants.

At sunset, in November, when the Pleiades
appear, after the arid rule of Canopus,
my rough herd moves in concert
to the stars of rain.

Bald Adham

Bald Adham, Jaham's sidekick, was a sleek
grease-monkey from Jizan, that hell
hole on the Red Sea where the cats
tiptoe with tails atilt down pitted streets.

In Jizan, cockeyed town, everything tilts:
The whitewashed minarets decline like dials
on sunstruck clocks, the windows lean
their woozy panes at angles to the lanes,
the alleyways are twisted with declivities,
and in the oil-smudged surf flamingos tilt
with stubby wings uplifted as in rough
supplication to some asymmetric god.

Bald Adham in his bandoliers of grease
hectored Jaham to join the Holy War.
Adham saw the infidel in every wing
nut and sprocket, sniffed the heretic
in air filters rounded by idolatry,
in barbaric typefaces on air-couriered crates,
blind steel impressed with bestial anagrams
in the Beelzububic lingo of the Yanks.
Tony the Tiger spelled the End of Days
when Dajjâl would rise up with all his hordes
to lick believers' blood out of their own skull-cups.
The infidel is everywhere, he growled. He spat
dreadful imprecations as he overhauled
staggered transmissions and sprained modulator valves.

Jaham humoured his friend. Theology, he thought,
was a tumor of reason caused by the *jinn*.
He loathed transcendence as he loathed the clap.
He wiped the sludgy sweat from Adham's brow
until his old pal's baldness glimmered like a dome
at dawn resplendent with sweet truth, a minaret
emerging from the dubious clouds of night.

He knew his friend's horizon was askew
for in the town that spawned him, by the sea,
even the smutty shorebirds must correct the sky.

Bald Adham Says his Prayers

At midnight Adham crawled out of bed
and held a loud palaver with the Lord
of both the worlds. He unrolled his prayer rug,
thinned to tatters where his forehead
rubbed against the fabric as he bowed,
and pitted where his supplicating knees
fulcrumed his prostrations. Adham kowtowed
melodically, both palms beside both ears,
with yips of praise and howls of accolade,
his brow abased and his hindquarters high,
and sang out words the centuries
that intervened between the Messenger and us
had scoured to such a shine
they glimmered with anonymity.
Adham never asked his Lord for anything.
His tongue coiled about each spittle-
burnished syllable with a quickened
lick of love, his prayer a cat
that purrs with praises as it brisks its pelt.

There was a pleasure for him in the nights
he lavished on invisible
blandishments and shadow lauds.
His prayer became a house
in which each window was an ardent vowel
lighting the casement that it then consumed.

And when he felt the night grow burdensome
Adham bawled a final cantillation
whose hot vehemence made the roof beams creak.
Muezzin of impetuous minarets,
he sobbed cadenzas that assailed the heights
to seduce God into daybreak once again.

Jaham Divines

Jaham listened to auguries and yarrow stalks.
He read the will of God from the groins of dunes.
The armpits of arroyos told him where
the lovingkindness of Allah had hid
groundwater for his camel calf to lap
out of the branded goblet of his palm.
He reverenced the knees of creosote
bushes and the shoulder blades acacias
promenade beneath the lustful moon.
He read the future from encrypted
messages the bones on badlands left.
He trusted in the alphabets of stars,
the syllabaries of the fretful clouds.

At night, when the hungry moon began
to howl, Jaham listened. He could swear
he heard the scritch of a black ant
upon the pumice of an ancient lake,
could hear the breathing of the ant,
could time its cadences, could calibrate
the secret collocation of its mandibles
as it prayed in darkness for the grain of light
it carried in its pincers to its lair.
Jaham felt his own heart start to beat
in subterranean clicketings of hope:
he tasted the rain in granaries of cloud
and learned the silos where the winds are stored.

An Old Poet Bites

When he was fourteen Jaham got
the mystic mantle of his poetry.
The luminescent prosody
of a dying master
came down to him one day.

Jaham paid a visit to the bard.
The bard was portly and avuncular,
nibbled on pears and pomegranates as
they chatted, but was failing fast.

When Jaham went to leave, the poet
crooked a plump index finger at him, beckoned
him to the bedside where he urged
Jaham to bend close, bend closer, near his mouth.

With unexpected vigor the old man
Sank two sharp incisors into the boy
—into his sweet and speechless mouth—
and fanged him like a sidewinder,
stabbing his mouth till the hot bite
brought blood. And then he said:

The only antidote is in the bite.

Jaham went home writhingly and learned to write.

Jaham on the Conquests of Childhood

North of a bottlecap lay Samarqand.
With pocketknives we divvied up the spoils.

With lances made of windshield wipers or of broken brooms
We hunted mighty Yazdegird to earth.
We cut his kingly throat, we stuck his head
On a creaking gatepost where his satraps stood.

East of a punctured inner tube there burned
The brazen furor of Heraclius.

West of the blear-eyed aggies in their pungent bag
We brought the terrible Berbers underfoot
And sailed on matchbox triremes through the Straits.

South of a slingshot made of forking twigs
And held together by a twanging band,
We saw the archipelagoes of the newborn day
And unimaginable peoples coursing there.

Beyond the tire pit Ecbatana shone.

Jaham and His Cat

The pink melodious ratchet of her tongue
Psalmodized as she hunched on Jaham's chest.
Jaham admired her reverence of repose,
The prayerful alertness of her ears,
The pierced opacity of her green eyes
Whose irises held aloof the more they shone,
Her silken dignity, the way she made
A pedestal of paw to rest upon
Behind a twitching balustrade of tail.

To drink he gave her pungent camel's milk
He bought at the Desert's Edge Convenience Store.
Jaham listened, he heard her chant Qur'an
In purr-cadenzas of complicit calm.
The cat sang *Allah Allah Allah*
And made her chant sound natural as breath.

Was she some subtle prophetess of sleep,
A disciple of our Prophet (may God
Pray for him!), who once had said:
People are sleeping;
When they die, they wake?

He remembered how Muhammad cut his cloak
Rather than dislodge a dozing cat.
All night he let her murmur on his breast,
All night her coiled contentment lulled his rest.

Jaham Serenades a Snake

O patterned psychopomp,
All spiral tail and curlicue of gait,
All accent-lashed, all circumspect of hip,
Teach me hollow inside hollow
Where the magnet mind can't follow!
Your hunch and crumple progress down a slope
Has the topple look of hope,
The spillgate promise of the brimming cup,
Even as you coil your selves down our thorny dunes,
Fumy as ectoplasm with an ambient
Emollience of sand.

                  I saw its whipping autograph
Surmount the idle and mellifluous stub
Of the tail. I saw the swallower swallowed in the loam
Hollow of itself as fingertip in fawn
Glove is gowned and fragrantly transformed.
I saw its virgule sassiness embrangle earth.
I thought,
Poor sheepskin! Poor certificate! But the nimble
Bureaucrat inverts itself while we
Salute a tail-tip from the Cherokee.

I know
Your snake's tongue semaphores some question
To us. Your sleek lip interrogates our air.
You know the hidden bodies of our families
For you have sucked their bones for prey.
You twined the eye sockets of my grand-dad's
Skull, you slid and you insinuated
Into the pelvis of my mother and my aunt, you
Circumambulated all the buried bones
The way a supple pilgrim throngs about
The midnight meteorite in the silver clasp
Of the Ka'ba

                    And if I cry aloud
Only the jointed rosary of your vertebrae
Is left for me to pray, forgetful

Supplicant, adoze in the warmth of the sun
From whose imperishable fingernails
The names of God will run
Like blacksnakes over stones.

The Baboons of Hada

The baboons of Hada love the heights.
High places let them contemplate
The sordid valleys they have left behind.
Along the scalded stones blue lizards lie,
Flatten themselves or pump their beaded throats.
But the baboons of Hada are aloof.
The baboons know the indifference of peaks;
Even their antics are deliberate;
Their skipping over crags has stateliness.

I like the way the baboons of the heights
Have colonized the coldest pinnacle,
Have softened and made stoical and sly
The summits where five stringy crows still wheel,
Have humorized abysses, made crevasses
Comical, vaudevilleaned the avalanche.
Now the sweet sisters groom their brothers' braids,
Old aunties coif the mustaches of nieces;
Their bright fastidious molars crackle mites.

And all the while one Abrahamic ape,
The dominant, the doge of his troupe,
Hunkers heraldic on a lip of stone.
His silvery Hamitic sideburns fluff
In the breezes of the heights. He shuts both eyes.
The patriarch of Hada shuts his eyes
And all around is sibilance and gust.
The scavenger baboons, consanguineous,
Plump down on their buttocks in the calm.

A sense of fullness rises with the dusk.
Five crows still quarrel at contested scraps
But the lord of foragers is throned in peace
Amid the frisky chittering of his kids.
The baboons wait until the rocks of heights
Become supernal in the full moon's light.

At nightfall the baboons of Hada sit
In chuckling circles where they contemplate
The radiant bottom of the risen moon.

(al-Ṭā'if, July 1997)

The Egyptian Vulture

> "Egyptian Vultures are well known as being
> the least discriminating of scavengers."
> —W. E. Cook, *Avian Desert Predators*

The Egyptian Vulture is the least
discriminating of the scavengers.
He sucks up eyeball juice of wildebeest
as though it were iced Bollinger.

He spreads a grey paté of rotted gnu
on a barfed-up bed of jungle turkey comb.
Raw rectum of gazelle is *cordon bleu*
yet how piously he dines, with plumed aplomb!

The stomach contents of some ripe giraffe
pleasure him more than freshly slivered truffles.
He stuffs his whole head in and you hear him laugh
as he snacks on gassy guts and belly ruffles.

Would you really call him *indiscriminate*?
True, his topknot is fouled with shit and bile
(unavoidable when you work your snout in straight
up the flyblown butt of some long-dead crocodile),

but see how he grooms himself when his chow is done:
he hangs his litigious pinions out to air,
he preens his turban till it's debonair,
he strops his beak in the Egyptian sun.

At the Ruins of Recollection

Bald Adham and Black Mary

Despite his orthodoxy Adham fell
for a cockeyed girl among the infidel.

Black Mary with her Abyssinian
mincing and her deftly fluttered dulcimer
she strummed all evening with a supple whir—

tortured him at his prayers. Callipygian
promise wafted from her rose-petal-seamed *'abaya*
and yet, she was uncleaner than a hound,
thick with fleas of heresy and ticks of doubt.

One night she offered him fresh-sliced papaya
on a silver tray. Her tattooed toes peeped out
under her hem. Adham sighed. He pawed the ground.
He snorted like a stallion led to stud.
Black Mary drew him down into the sweet pink mud
behind the body shop and wrapped him in her veils.
In the name of God! he roared and lipped her breasts.
Praise to the Creator! Adham thundered as her nails
dug into the bare flesh of his back and sinuous gusts
of some Djibouti perfume cloaked his throat, his nose.
Glory Glory be to God! Bald Adham stammered
as he mounted Black Mary and then entered her,
a drugged bee asprawl in a nectarous rose.

Let me instruct you in the Path of Truth! he yammered
but Black Mary wound him in a silken blur,
enlaced and wove and filamented him in silicate
strands more delicate
than the gossamer
flounces orioles confect on summer boughs.

Adham could not extricate
his limbs from hers, his breath from the drowse
of her breath on his throat. And so they lay,
orthodox and infidel, until the white thread of day—
that moiré glimmer on the satin-stitch of night—
could just be distinguished by its own merged light.

Adham Sings of Internal Combustion

The crankshaft sucks the piston to its brink
And then the camshaft opens up the valves.
I love to let the anointed piston sink
Down towards the flywheel in the engine block.

The air-brimmed fuel is drawn into the cylinder
And at the last plunge of the piston's strike
The intake valves fall closed and so surrender.
The crankshaft slides the piston through the cylinder
And enters in and occupies and salves
The block with dizzy vapors from the chamber
Where lightning-frictioned sweet combustion tinders
The spark plugs' effervescence of ignition.

I love the vaporous and thrummed cognition
The engine block surrenders as it comes
To full exhaustion in the flywheel's spoke.

I love the crankshaft's spin just when emission
Kindling the engine's cycle re-engenders
Propulsion while the crankshaft hones its screws.

O there's a cadence to the slicked machine!
There is a sweet-greased music to the cylinder!

I love the snug piston whose dense gasoline
Ambrosial with oxygen now renders,
In frothy plunges, as the flywheel spins,

Strummed spasms of combustion to the engine block.

Love Among the Dunes

When Jaham fell in love his skin became
Xylophonic. Each fingertip would ping,
Each dimple vocalize till all his body chimed.
His toenails clicked their little castanets,
His ankles and patella cadence-clacked,
His nipples pizzicattoed with a taut
Epidermal anthem of delight,
His piccolo of penis piped its glee,
And even his shy balls in their goathair sack
Blipped like muffled bugles when he walked.

His tongue alone was thronged with silences.
His mouth was deader than a soldered flute,
His teeth chatterless as a sprained harmonium.
Even his garrulous eyeballs had turned dumb.

But when love came to him, that leopard-whelp
With dark lope and both wild eyes
Like pristine puddles where blue cyclones loom,
His very gooseflesh crooned to the dunes

In phosphor aureoles of synaptic song.

Jaham Deciphers the Script of Insomnia

O stars that calligraph my sleeplessness!
All night your delicate nibs have filigreed
The virgin blackness of the southern sky
With sly epistles in a chancery hand,
And I lie open-eyed, heart athud, my mind
Straining to decipher your shrewd strokes.
I see a sudden swoop-shaped vowel
Gild the parchment of a scrolling cloud,
But then heat lightning puffs the page
With flocks of full-stops and I stammer there,
My palate thistled by the scripted sky.

Night is a block of solid black,
Night is a cube, a *ka'ba*, a chunk
Of another world behind our world.
Night is a holy dense irreducible
Pebble draped in a sumptuous covering,
Needlepointed with the consonants of God,
Birdwinged with startled vowels.

And under the Ptolemaic helices of heaven
The moon is a pudgy scribe who dabs
Unctuous letters on the pumice clouds.
A lazy, lolling, word-infested scribe
Whose fingers, disciplined in indolence,
Stipple bright *fathas*, opulent *dammas*,
Kasras piercing as the fang of dawn,
Along the vellum of the midnight sky.

Sleeplessly I follow the plump moon's reed
Pen as it dwindles and then upswells
And I hate the fat moon with a fierce affection,
I hate how he doodles on the anthracite
Immaculate darkness with his stub of a pen,
One studious drop of radiance
Quilling its fertile tip.

Mrs. Jaham

"In my youth I married a ghoul
Who resembled a gazelle."
—al-Jahiz, *The Book of Animals*

One morning Bald Adham glimpsed
The naked foot of Jaham's wife as she
Slipped him a cup of coffee through the flap
Of the connubial tent. Despite the numerous
Bangles that gave voices to her wrist,
Adham saw her foot was slipperless
And thick with a downy pelt of blackest fur.

And Adham understood then that his pal
Had married not a gazelle but a ghoul
And that his power as a poet
Came from the uncanny
Cloaked in a kitchen robe.

Bald Adham Falls into Heresy

Bald Adham said one day:
God is an amputee,
A disincarnate Hand
Aslant the sky It papered and drew taut

He wouldn't recant but later claimed:
God is a sandstorm made of body parts,
A casual, agglomerated Thing.
Yes, God is a Thing, he said,
An object all direction but dimensionless.

Still, God must have a bottom, said he, for
He sits upon a Throne . . .

The next day he said: God is a foot.

Jaham asked him, "Does God have ten toes like us?"

Adham answered him: The Almighty has
Only ten toes, like us, but they are in

Infinitudes of foot.

Adham Overhauls an Old Caprice

Bald Adham used a threaded damper puller
To coax the hub from the end of the crankshaft.
He took out the pulley retaining bolts
And then withdrew the breather pipes from the rocker covers.
He pondered the hairpin clip
At the bell crank, then carefully
Removed that too. He swabbed the mating
Surfaces of the cylinder head and rubbed them clean
With loving swipes of rag and a growled out prayer.

"My little *ḥubâra*, my sweet sand grouse,"
He crooned, "You have grown old, like me!"
He diagnosed his body as he diagnosed
The engine of an old Caprice. He knew
His timing chains were clanking on overtime,
His dowel-pin chamfer was a catastrophe,
And even his camshaft sprocket, once his pride,
Wobbled when he floored the pedal now.
He remembered with a blush beneath his grease
Days when his steering knackle and his
Stabilizer bar required
No pry-tool for their maintenance.

Now, left to overhaul this elderly V-8,
He plunged his surgical fingers, gloved in sludge,
Into the torque-stunned heart of the engine block.
"My dove," he sang, "My antelope,"
As he dotingly installed
New valve-cover grommets that the Infidel
Had docked at Jeddah just two weeks before.

"Beloved," he hummed, "when your lugnuts gleam again
We'll tame the turnpikes and outrun our rust."

The engine shivered. Adham felt
The whomping heart fire at his fingertips.
He sensed how purringly his own

Combustion chamber filled again
With the gleam of fuel.

Bald Adham kissed his grease gun and oil filter wrench
And he praised the Lord Who pricks the dead to life.

Hubble-Bubble

On Fridays Jaham smoked his hubble-bubble.
He stuffed the bowl with hashish smuggled in
Beneath the floorboards of a Lebanese
Watermelon trucker named Fu'ad.
He held a smolder to the fragrant lump.
Opulent bubbles wallowed as he drew
Columns of smoke into his cloudy mouth.
Jaham dream of houris as he puffed,
Of breasts like goblets where his thirst might sip
Honeydew from rosy nipples, dreamed of thighs
Ambrosial with the juices of desire
Where he might stallion all paradise
And ride his wives, Jaham a lightning-bolt
Piercing the fleecy negligees of clouds.

In pungent billows of aerated smoke
The hubble-bubble fed his reveries.
The more he smoked the more he felt himself
No dreamer but the insubstantial smoke
The pipe tossed with a chuckle to the air.

The hubble-bubble was umbilical
And swaddled him in cauls
Of intimate myrrh. On
Spanked-up cushions of upholstered smoke
Jaham inhaled the familiar, the much-loved
Alleyways of towns he'd never seen.

There the souks of paradise had opened:
Transfigured merchants were unspooling hanks
Of spangled fabrics woven by the hands
Of invisible children laughing silkily.

The Jinn

have an oily railyard lantern flare
of equivocal blaze. Sometimes, when so
inclined, the coastal jinn give off a musk
animal glow such as cat fur produces on a rainy day.
They are fond of tall tales and they cluster round
the burner when the *bunn* is being roasted.
As the magic whiff
of freshly toasted coffee beans climbs up
the hairy wall of the tent and as tranquillity
glints in the smug crimson of the coal,
the jinn begin to gloss the words of men.

Their speech is an incised shape of silence, an intaglio,
in which the word is not a single, schisted bloc
of sense, like ours, but guards its pristine
opacity and is impossible
for any dragoman to approximate.

We can only
struggle to imagine their colloquies,
all consonant and *sukûn*,
a gravity of gesture tinged by the fire they are—
ingot-malleable, nugget-plush, pyritic and aureate—
and yet, for all their clang,

perorating and impulsive as a flame.

Jaham Sings of the Fear of the Moon

The moon is thin with fear,
the delicate moon is thinner than despair.

The fear of the moon is the fear of the hare
curved in its burrow when the fox is near.

The fear of the moon is the fear of the fog
(The fog is afraid of the fox and the dog

and the moon is afraid of all three.)
The moon is a thorn in midnight's tree.

The moon is thin as the edge of a cry,
as fine as the side of a word.

The thin moon hides in the dark of my eye.
Night-hidden I heard

its thinness crackle like the stalks of fall
before the hail comes and the first stars fall.

Night-hidden I heard its thin feet run
away from the golden horror of the sun.

Jaham's Dream Camel

When the dawn is splashed with white like an old man's skull
I set out on my camel, full-blooded and freshly branded.
Her ears resemble fronds on the naked palm
Or the myrtle that towers high above the reeds.
Her hoof is a downturned bowl,
Black-rimmed as inscriptions on a faience cup.

My mare surpasses the aim of the widest eye.
She's quicker than water to run down polished hills.
She's quicker than heart-piercing thought
Or the twisting eye-flickers of a man in doubt.

My Sherari camel is hellfire itself.
She blazes unceasingly, a tamarisk
Of flame stoked by the winds of the Great Nafûd.

She is a falcon trained to the rule
That lays on the thick-gloved hand of the falconer
A harsh and stropping lash of punishment.

My camel is swifter than the skeptic's look.
She plunges the way rain plunges into a well.
She is skittery like the glowering auger's eye
Glimpsing phantoms in damp-clodded soil.

She flies like a woman terrified
Of her own desire
And who yet hunts down the torture of her desire.
She never flies except toward spouting blood.

She pierces the north.

She pierces the south.

—after the Caliph Ibn al-Mu'tazz (murdered 908)

Jaham Travels West to Khemisset Oasis

The lathing of erosion on the hills
Has whittled away all angularities and left
These womanly declivities and swells:

An eloquence of shoulders in the slopes
Of the olive groves, velvety
Insinuations that spool down
From clavicles of cherished terraces.
The leaves the olives proffer to the light
Have a gravity of silver in their flourishes.
And the trees receive the footprints of the breeze
That hotly steps across their canopies
Like children when their mother wipes their faces—
Mild but definitive.

                    The hills are sofa-brown
And plush with vinyl accents where one field's
Stitched to a neighbour's. And there are cryptic
Cicatrices which a plow
Impressed into the old recycled soil and these
Faint scars pale at sunset with a ritual
Patterning: henna-tinted, dim tattoos.

Beyond the bosomy embedded sides
Of the hills the sternness of sierras
Alerts the light. Dusk twinkles lethally
From riptooth peaks which guard the sea beyond
Like shattered bottle-bits on garden walls.

At the Ruins of Recollection

"Traces that speak not . . ."
—Zuhayr

I grieve for Mulaybid
Now a scramble of ruins.
In ochre doorways the spider
Has set up her loom.
In fragrant chambers
Where giggling virgins henna'd their fingers
The scorpion nests her spawn.
In curtained bedrooms where the bridegroom once
Laid bare the eager nipples of his bride
The jackal whelps her pups.
And from the tilting chimneys
The scribal owl recites the lineage
Of children with their slate-
Scratched signatures who all
Have vanished from the benches of the school.

I grieve for the evenings of Turayf
Whose voices wove
A fabric that the crackle
Coals of the tamarisk
Threaded with its aromatic
Banter to a vivid silk
That mantled us. Families
Squatted there with crimson
Shadows of companionship
Softening faces that the wind
Had carved, with palms
The sands had seamed
Made affable to the clasp of coffee cups.

I grieve for the voices lost
In the sift of recollection,

Beyond Mulaybid where the harsh
Ever-seething ridges of the Dahna rise,
Past Wadi Hanifah where the wild
Goats browse, past the smudge of storm-
Strewn campsites whose inscriptions now my eyes
Cannot decipher on the fire-scrawled cooking stones.
I grieve for the moons we once together watched.
I grieve for the moon
The unremembering sun has bled to death.

Last Things

Ramadan

A jackass was braying in the date palm grove.
By the starry watering hole
Goats were browsing on the fronds
Of the young palms. The billygoat,
His mufti's beard curved like the letter *lâm*,
Clattered upon the mud brick parapet
And studied Jaham with his oblong eyes.
The mud-baked palaces of the emirs,
The picked bones in the cinders,
The freshly sooted surfaces of the stones,
Moved Jaham more than chives in early spring
When the badlands glimmer with their bright sharp shoots.

Ramadan fell in the summer of that year.
By day they didn't eat or drink or smoke.
They didn't unhook the tent flaps of their wives.
All day they sat in the shade of the roof
Or dozed on cushions with their hands
Propping their chins. Remembrance came
(through expiations that the sand itself
learned in the ages before God made man)
And instructed them to parch
Pious routine out of their usual bones.

When Jaham heard the call to prayer he rose
And muttered, *Lethal poison*! But when
The jackass brayed and the pariah dogs
All fell to howling he exclaimed
These are my true muezzins!
And he prayed to God until his temples rang.

Jaham Praises

". . . in prayer it is recommended that one say, 'O
Lord of heavens and earth!' and not 'O Lord of
dogs and swine,' even though He is their Lord."
—Ibn Manzur, *Lisan al-'arab*, vi:67.

Lord, You are holy in
bloody napkins and the mouths of flies.

I praise You, Lord, not only in the disprized
pig but in the shit that cakes its trotters and its rump.

I praise You, Lord, at execution grounds
and in the neighbourhoods of tanneries. I
praise You in the tripes and in the bowels.

I praise You in the mandibles of bedbugs
that nip my ass and make me rise at night.
And when I rise, I make my orisons
to You, Ineffable, who gleam in turds
and tumors, in bunions and in lesions and in scabs.

Poets bore the peacocks with glozening
encomia. They wear the roses away.
I praise the muck
where sowbugs drowse.
I praise the things
You fashioned out of
more than love—out of Your
secret pleasure in the obdurate: Your
tough nuggets of refusal, all the lost

atoms You abandoned at the Fall.

Jaham on the Difficult Beauty of the First White Hair

What is lovelier than the dark
when it draws the heavy curtains of the day
and beds the sun in cushions of black cloud?
A passion of blackness coronates the heads
of the young and blackness gives their skulls
that onyx glossiness.

                    Today I found
My first white hair. How could my light
be dying when my heart
is twined by black strands to the farthest star?

As always in distress I took my refuge in
the verses of the classics where I read
what Sharif al-Radi wrote of his first white hair:

Time rubs the swordblade free of tarnishes
Youth's impetuous loveliness imposes.

Caliph of Confusion

There is a tiny speck in Jaham's eye
Where the Caliph of Confusion rents a room.
The Caliph is insane and loves costume.
One day a nuncio, the next an Albanian spy.
He is no principle. He is an imp.
He enacts the spasm in the woof of time
But stands for nothing at all beyond a crimp
In comprehension, that small, sublime
Stammer we enunciate when sense breaks down
And the smug palate and the thuggish tongue
Baffle their Delphic and lubricious truths
To stuttered stillness.

          When he was young
Jaham's eye was a perfectly pure, nut-brown
Orb without a single speck and his strong
Throat sang with all the certified youths
Of his tribe. The Caliph was his Iblîs—
A nip of darkness in the skin of the light,
The sly flea that itches the lobes of peace—
But he taught him how to navigate the night.

A Duet with the Wolf

"Many's the sable-grey honey-gatherer, no friend of mine,
I've called to my fire at midnight, and he came to me . . ."
—Al-Farazdaq

In the crackle light of his coals Jaham
caught the fire-shine of back-teeth.
He smelled wolf's breath.

"My wolf," he announced, "I'm holding a 30.06!"
To his surprise the wolf sang back with a rhyme:
O please let me snuggle up to your fire of sticks!

Jaham pondered and then improvised
and each of his impromptus the wary wolf revised:
"My wolf, I am old but my eye, though bleared, sees far.
With a single shot I can drill a tossed dinar."

The wolf commenced a counter-strum like a seven-stringed
        guitar:
My pelt's a shred, my ribs poke out, my pads are blisters.
Early senility has stippled my whiskers.
Jaham's rejoinder sidled like a twister:
"My molars shone like mosque lamps brimmed with blessed oil
and now they jut like blackened chassis from a junkyard soil.
Once they were high beams backed with lambent foil
and now glom darkly like some burnt-out fumarole . . ."

The wolf began a half-suppressed, resentful boil:
Your teeth! My arrogant fangs are worn down as the curbs
where knackered camels piss, they are lonely as suburbs
in bankrupt desert developments, they're feeble as the blurbs
festooning failed potboilers with inflated verbs . . . !

Jaham (whom no braggadocio perturbs)
feinted fiercely then and pointed to his brows:
"My eyebrows once were prickly as iron rasps

whose stiff aplomb no brusque khamsin can dowse,
my temples were the robust hasps
of teak-paneled glove compartments, my . . ."

The wolf untous-
led his tongue and contralto'd this response:
My eyes, once bright as a fire of thorns in hell,
are wizened as waterskins at a scum-choked well.
But blurred as they are, my eyes can pounce
and calibrate my supper to the final ounce,
and I dine on both believer and on infidel!

Jaham cocked his rifle. He felt strength return,
as though lament were fuel for old age to burn.
But the wolf inched closer in that fiery solitude
and began to keen:
I who whelped my thousands am now Time's eunuch,
castrato of vicissitude,
a mothball-pasha in a tattered tunic,
howling in his hebetude,
and forced to share the fire with a versifying mechanic,
I who once commanded the stony wastes of Thamûd!

The wolf stood up from his hollow by the fire.
He threw back his whitened snout.
A cracked complaint teetered from his throat
while his ribs swelled like a wheezing concertina
and his final molars clittered like a string of beads.
As he threaded the desert air with a yipping sorrow,
that night by the coals where they bickered to soothe one
        another,
in his howl, so quavering and prosodic, Jaham could hear
the history of a life given to the anonymous wind
and the history of his own days,
gnawed to a bone of song.

Adham Atones

"Wash me of my sins with ice water and hail!"
Adham beseeched, "Scrub me with frost and thorn!"
The sand could not scour Adham of his sins
And in the holy month of Rajab he rose up.
"I'll lick the iron," he informed Allah.
These fits came on him every year or so.

He packed his saddle bags with figs and cheese.
He ambled eastward, heading for Liwa',
And as he rose, he haggled with Allah:
"Don't cool the sun for me, that ghoul!
See how she spreads her furnace-lips! Ha!
Send 'Izzat, send me Lât, send all your fiends
To winkle the rot from my soul's cavities . . . !"

He thirsted for abasement as he raged.
He wanted to surmount the prayer that's just
Pleasurable calisthenics for the tongue.
He wanted to hold the mortifying knife
Close to his ribcage. He wanted to puff alive
That ash-encumbered ember that we call the heart.

The Sweat of Adham

Jaham wondered at the sticky sweat
That collected on the forehead of his friend.
He kissed the sweat off with his lips
As it sprouted in fat drops on Adham's skin
And trickled to the corners of his eyes
And ran along his cheekbones to his chin.
The sweat of death was on his oldest friend.
The more the sweat steamed from his pores
The stiller Adham lay. He was a well
Evaporating in the suck of noon.
He was a waterhole where vagabonds
Scrounge the final droplets with their tongues.
He was a wadi where the spring cascades
Parch as they race among the grains of clay.
He lay there on his sodden bed
And all the veins along his bald head
Writhed and swelled, they grappled
With his blood that still rebelled.

Jaham plucked the sprigs of sweat away.
He dabbed at the panic in Bald Adham's eyes
With cool caresses and with gnomic lullabies
And he chanted in his soft falsetto voice
A solace of surahs from the August Book.
Adham gazed at him, then said,
"I can't find Allah by my jugular . . ."

When Adham died, freshets ran
Out of his eyelids and his bristly ears,
Out of his caverned nostrils and his lips.
His shoulder-blades were sopping with his death.
And from his bright skull to his drenching toes
Adham turned into a salt flat where the sun
Hacks its mirages out of dead men's bones.

Adham in the Torments of the Tomb

There was a coziness in being dead
Adham had not expected. Nestled in a shroud,
his head towards Mecca and his restless hands
girdled at his waist, with several
cubic feet of sand heaped over him,
he felt himself a kernel in a ripening date.
He heard his last friends overhead
gossip and sob beside his modest grave.
He heard Black Mary whoop and ululate.
He strained to catch the panegyric words
they lavished on his dwindling memory
and if his blood still ran he would have blushed.
He gloated in the praises that seeped down
into the snuggled darkness of his tomb.
But as their voices faded, as their steps
receded from his final resting place,
Adham felt a stab of grief and then
the grave began to tighten, his tomb
began to squeeze, he felt himself a coin
pinched in the bony talons of a miser.
He tried to shout, his mouth was bridled shut.
He tried to move, his feet were fettered fast.
He tried to weep, his eyelids were weighed down
by double pebbles in death's discipline.
The sand was famished and he felt it suck—
styptic and invincible and alkaline—
till all that was a river in him died.

Two sudden angels now began to worm
into his confines. *Call me Munkar*,
said the first. He looked like a religious cop,
all barbed-wire beard and dim salacious eye.
My name's Nakir, the second said. He had a bland
turban speckled with food stains on his skull
like a lazy mufti chewing a bent toothpick.

Each had a ball-point pen
clipped to one pocket of his nylon robe
but their wings were down at heel
and needed servicing.

Welcome to Barzakh! chirruped plump Nakir
but Munkar piped up with, *What do you believe?*
Adham for the first time in his death
thought, *I believe it's hellish here.*
I believe in the sun and in the moon and stars.
I believe in the beauty of well-serviced racing cars . . .
But he responded, *I do testify*
there is no God but God
and Muhammad is God's messenger!

Not bad, said Nakir but Munkar pressed on:
Tell us, he wheedled, *about God's attributes.*
Are they substratal with His essential Self
or superadded to His essence, hmmmm?
Adham pondered that and then replied,
I think that I'll be many moons down here!

Munkar began to jab and Nakir knelt
on Adham's belly and he pummeled him.
Both angels worked him over most methodically
with kidney pokes and left hooks to the ribs
until he howled,
His attributes are additives to God's own fuel!

See what a little jostling can do? said Munkar.
They gave Adham D+
but he had passed. He'd passed and yet,
it would be many moons before he went
over the razor's edge and the rim of flame.
It would be nestled eons till he stepped
out of the tightness of his resting place.
It would be epochs of impatience
(tucked like an ancient seed inside the husk
of his sand-scooped tomb) till Adham walked

out of the earth again, with all the dead,
to glimpse the farthest lotus tree and sip
from the cooling rivulets of Salsabil.

Jaham Curses

After Bald Adham perished Jaham howled
at heaven for seven days and seven nights.
He damned the arrogance of destiny but
Mrs. Jaham said, *Think of Ayyûb!*
Think of his long-suffering and welcome fate!

Jaham rose up from his place of grief and spoke:
I damn fate with my words,
I damn him with my fingers and my toes,
I damn him with my eyelids and my chin
and I damn him with my dick and testicles!
I say: You scurvy and marauding cur,
you rank fox who scarfs our darlings down,
I hate the way you grind up all our bones
and punch out all our teeth with slingshot stones.
I hate how you vandalize our last good looks
and even rifle our sorry savings books.
You spit out all our bones the way an owl
disgorges the fur and bones of little mice
after he's sucked a bellyful of blood!

Mrs. Jaham got nervous. *Hush*, she said,
Hush! She knew how slyly destiny
will sniff at the keyholes and the window joists,
how avidly blind fate will press its ear
to the thin walls and strain to catch a curse,
how it eavesdrops on the sentences of men
and scavenges among their careless words,
how it hunches to listen, just below the lip,
and hides in the pleats of gowns to pounce upon
the mutinous flinches of our stubborn souls.

Her soft cool paw she set on Jaham's mouth,
her breasts that smelled of earth in early spring
she bared for his solace. He could taste
wild onion, colocynth, and chicory
in the mother-covenant of her spurting milk.

Allah Answers Jaham in the Days of Dust

Have you ever
studied the annelations in the grub worm's weird
caparison? Have you ever listed
the bristles in the cacomistle's beard
or numbered its whiskers?
Do you know where the bandicoot
whelps her bandicootlets? Can you recruit
the fennec, the jerboa or the giant clam?
I am that I am I am:
That is enough for you
(you don't even know the secrets of the kinkajou!).

Consider the camel, *My*
design entirely. Consider how
her nubile nostrils can
asperge the sand: I came up
with that. Her popular hump
that wobbles as she strides
is *Mine* as well, and the affluence
of fat she larders in that hump
speaks with greasy eloquence of *My*
sovereign kindness to the sons of men.
Consider her virginal and lustrous eye
balls pavilioned with delicate fly-whisks
of lash, and the pools of her enigma
in amber irises that narrow as she ruminates
her cud. I am justly proud of this
invention of the camel. Consider her!
Consider her monarchical tuft
of tail, her ingot hoofs that ring
across the badlands and can spark a flint!

Consider how My camel-creature
rolls her lips back from her yellow teeth
and roars in her jubilance
whenever she sniffs a carrot or a watercourse!

Jaham, consider! It was I who shaped you
like a loving owlet on a sundown tree
who whistles hosannas to the stars of night.
I fashioned you like a jackal dog whose yips
buff the roughest stones and make them glad.
And I will hold you always in the covert of My eye.

Jaham Says Adham's Beads

This was his rosary of olive wood
Whose ninety-nine black beads hang from a cord.
He bought it on the pilgrimage, while still a child,
And it always looped down from his grimy hand.

The rosary's repose is serpentine.
It coils in its fat black coils in asp-encirclings
And viper-rippling rings
And when I pick it up the dark discs click

Between my fingers as I breathe the names
God gave Himself before the world began:
Creator, Fashioner, Immortal One,
Enduring, Living, Mighty, Merciful . . .

The strand yields to my impatient hand
With staccato softness of its vocatives:
Victorious, Compassionate, O Listener!
Resurrecting and Extinguishing, Unique!

But I pray better with the voiced
Beads of the rosary, and not with names.
My supplication's in my fingertips
That slides the awed wood down the hidden thread.

The Junkyard Vision of Jaham

In paradise the smell of engine oil
Will undercut the roses. The carburetors
Of Eden will distract the seraphim,
Those jukebox lutanists in phosphate trees.
The vaporous hush of essences
At the pinging pump will cauterize
The contusions of love, and the houris all
Will bask on velveteen and naugahyde
Bucket seats in a Russian Leather breeze.

The camshafts of heaven will outlive the axle trees.
The music of the manifolds will gown the clouds.
I see the black-seamed fingertips of the mechanics
On the copper-coloured keys of their accordions
And hear the ditties of the pit-stops pool.
The music of paradise will be shirt-sleeved and cool
And brandish red bandannas of rough flannel.
The integrity of metals will marmorealize
Fleeting affections yet be various.
Amber oils will coronate chrome impulses
And be steadfast at last.

                The dark order
Of the mechanisms of heaven will be intricate
And unending, bedewed with rich grease
And yet, withal, imbued by the love
Of couplings and black
Gaskets, the grit of the known
Lingeringly delivered back to innocence.

Jaham Plans for the Disposal of his Remains

After the sun has sucked my last breath out
And stripped away the spittle from my lips
And blotted out the blackness of my eyes,
After the bony sun has bled me dry
And parched my skin of shoulder and of thigh,

After the wind has teazled out my hair
And whisked all music from my gritted chin
And pinched my loincloth and my BVDs
And dusted off the last speck of my sighs,

After the sands have filed my bones down fine
And buffered fingernails and toenails smooth
And scrimshawed all the ivory in my teeth,

After the rain has rinsed my sockets out
And racked my ribcage like a snooker set
And rivered all my sweat and semen down
Into the fatherless and fainting sand,

Offer my remnants to these modest friends:
The scarab and the jackal dog.

Let the vocal dog with scavenger address
Disarticulate my skeleton
And gnosh and knacker all my little bones
In midnight yapperies of his furred confrères.
Then let the scarab roll her frugal turds
Into one dark and compact ball of dung,
Let the beetle roll me in a fuming sphere
Across the dunes into a bramble's hug
And give back to the molecules I was
What thankfulness a thorn owes to the sun.

Jaham's Last Words

The imam was preaching when he read the verse:
Everything is perishing except His face.

The verse had always startled Jaham secretly.

The flies are perishing in bowls of milk.
The mice are dying in their labyrinths.
The heels of pilgrims with that darkly rosy
Rim of skin that glimmers when they bow
Are perishing, as are their vivid hands,
Their kisses, and their singing salutations,
The puffs of ochre dust their sandals plume.
Even the sun is dropping in its den.

As he was perishing himself
The cloudy poet said
The two lines that made his epitaph:

I love everything that perishes,
Everything that perishes entrances me.

V

DAYBREAK AT THE STRAITS

For my brother Alan

The Jewel Box

For Norm Sibum

I have not done with you, I have not done,
Dear Presences, who live on in the spun
braids of gold in the silk jewel box, who glance
at me from clumsy cameos, who dance
out of lurid corals or a split earring,
whose throats I summon to the supple string
where the oily pearls of buried evenings burn,
whose flesh I taste on my own lips in the sleek
surfaces of onyx or the bleak
blurred filigree some dutiful son brought back
from the gold-sellers' souk, the lightning-crack
in the brooch.

I have not done with your memories
who wreathe around me still, whose reveries
would smother me, dear loving vampires
whom imagination and my own desires
conjure out of gems and gold and paste.

Our ancestors are stronger than the taste
of some abandoned attar we still find
back of the jewel box where sweet shadows wind
remembrance out of fragrance until our tongues
burn like the first air breathed into newborn lungs.

I.

What the Snow Was Not

The snow was not liver-spotted like a gambler's
Hands. It did not reflect
Violet abrasions at the hubs of wheels
Or the well-glossed ankles of policemen.

The snow did not mimic flamingo rookeries
Or bone-stark branches where the spoonbills nest.
It had no single tint when it negated gold.
The snow was not duplicitous like arc

Lamps at sunrise that encairn the curbs
In lavender melodics. Snow did not web
The hands of women with their sudden hair
Electric-trellised in a blue downdraft.

The snow did not consume the eager mouths
Of children. It did not inhabit the skimming owl's
Concavity of surveillance and it did not flock
In grackle-shadows near the eaves of courts.

When you endow the snow with what it's not—
Mere shivering crystals blown by January
Over the squares in frosty negatives—
The snow becomes a god and nothing's lord.

Another Thing

To live in the body like a nervous guest;
To be confined in fingers and in feet;
To swing on the pendulum of what to eat;
To be subject to south and east and west . . .

Behind my skullbone lives another thing
That fidgets anxiously as I barge by,
That swivels skyward its chameleon eye
For the interests in the twitches of a wing.

My inmost dweller is predacious root;
Ransacks reality for steadfastness;
Adores the constancy of all dark stars;
Refuses thirst and thrives upon the brute
Benedictions of the wolf and lioness;
Loves the futility of fountains; preens scars.

Ant-Lion

Beneath your shoe soles an illusion smooths
The loose lank sandgrains into cavities
So exquisitely cocked that if you tease
Their edges with a straw the funnel seethes

Suddenly under to blank avalanche.
I saw a plodding ant's insouciance
Topple it over in a scramble-dance
Down down down into the clench

Of the ant-lion—Chaplinesque
Assassin of the sand, snug predator,
Larval hunter with a gladiator
Lunge of needle-mandibles, burlesque

Doodlebug, we called it, to domesticate
Terror made tiny, mayhem minusculed.
Below our eyes its drab precision ruled
Lilliputian worlds with silicate

Strategies, glint-facades of fright.
And sometimes when the ambushed day
Bleedingly withdrew to slumberous grey,
I heard my heartbeat striking in the night.

In dream sometimes the cliff-brink of the world,
That zigzag fracture of hurt porcelain
That leads beyond the darkness of the brain,
Funnels and shimmies, woozies to a hurled

Helter-skelter of ankles and shrill clothes
Upended, and we paw, in a fierce crawl,
Bare air, eyes dragged upward as our bodies fall,
Somersaulted, with heart-stopped mouths.

And if our fall were only infinite,
If falling were our pleasure and our grace,

If our momentum obviated place,
If our descent were indeterminate . . . !

What taloned nightmare grips us in the wild
Spiral of sleep? What ripped awakening?
What busy, greedy, inconspicuous thing?
What barely fledged phantasm of a child?

The ant-lion shrugs aside its camouflage,
Ruthless as a consumer elbows near
With upraised boning knife to shear
Something for that deep-freeze in the garage.

In dream we flutter above everyone.
In dream we Ixion the darkened sun.
Under our shoes a pinch of sand holds night—
Darkness puppeteered by appetite.

Dicie Fletcher

Whene'er, along the ivory disks, are seen,
The filthy footsteps of the dark gangrene;
When caries comes, with stealthy pace to throw
Corrosive ink spots on those banks of snow—
Brook no delay, ye trembling, suffering fair,
But fly for refuge to the dentist's care.
—Solyman Brown, *Dentologia: a Poem on the*
Diseases of the Teeth (1833), Canto Four

Πεῖρεν ὀδόντων
—Homer, *Iliad* xvi, 405.

"I have a horror of unconsciousness," she said.
She refused the nitrous oxide mixed with oxygen
(that still was new in 1881).
"Let me come clear-eyed unto Calvary,"
Dicie Fletcher, teacher of Classics, said,
hands braced against chintz armrests while she watched
Dr. Diore's lancing eye,
cool blue sun in incandescent sky,
assay each tooth-tap as he inch-
wormed nearer, nearer and still
nearer to that flinching place
where her sick tooth pulsed with pain.

"Would you reduce me to the mere *insensible*,"
she remembered, now, to her horror, having said.
"I tell you this, I disapprove of all
nepenthe. True propriety
must objurgate Lethean balm."
O now, how she cursed those chill
Ciceronian cadences of hers!

The bad tooth
seemed to shrink back like a guilty thing.
"They do some tiptop things these days

with hippopotamus," Dr. Diore drawled.
"It's all the thing—*ivory swaged with gold*!"
He saw the same old Dicie he had known
and hankered for for years. Since grammar school.
He shivered picturing her virginal
pale flesh swaddled inside stays and straps,
a woman barricaded behind her clothes
(and was he not the man to lay her siege?).
And Dicie looked at him, saw him up close.
His muttonchops were snarled with bloody flecks.
His jowl was peppered with old smallpox pits.
She remembered him as a small and shiftless boy—
now he'd got an office of his own, now
his thick and stubby fingers reeked of clove.

Her neckveins pounded and her temples rang.
And when Dr. Diore touched the culprit tooth
she writhed against the brimming of the hurt
that wrung out fiery teardrops from her eyes.
The Cross. O the Crown of Thorns . . .
faded from her, faded!

                    Peiren odonton . . .

Homer was the true Evangelist.
That's what she taught her boys.
Homer did not assuage, met doom
head-on. Uncoddled by all gospels, he
only held out hard pebble-phrases
for the agonized to suck. Yes, *peiren: drove*
("Aorist, boys? Who can tell me about this verb?")
"Patroclus *drove* the spear *between the teeth*—
odonton—of Thestor, son of Enops. He
gaffed the charioteer out of his chariot
like a bullfrog on a pole.") The doctor
whooped, "We've got it now!" ("Genitive
plural, that *omega*, boys, Homer's own
words, chilly as ivory, aloof to pain.")
She felt the bulldog bite of the clamp.

She moaned and Dr. Diore stroked her brow.
"O my, my, yes, the *torture of the forceps*," he consoled
(O how he wanted this woman, wanted her here and now!).

When a dark oak is cracked by cyclonic wind
and its lashed branches flail in the shrill black air
and the whole of heaven eddies with laceration
while under the skreegh of wind the herdsman hears
acorns pittering the rain-pocked soil
with palpitant volleys, gatling-gravel-pings,
so Dicie heard, from deep inside her skull,
how the tormenting third molar grunted, squeaked,
then twitter-stumbled like a stub of chalk
scraped across a blackboard to a shriek,
and she blubbered as the thick-embedded roots
tore at her gums till all at once,
with a popping suck it clopped into the dish
and rattled there, long-rooted, flung to defeat,
like Thestor when the quick
Patroclus hooked him down to black
Acheron and the terrible darkness came upon his eyes.
"Some alveolar mutilation . . . ," droned the doc.
(Tenderly his left hand brushed her throat!)

The cruelty of remembered Greek
came to her help. Grammar, that
propriety of all well-measured speech,
comforted even the mouth too torn to speak.
Didn't our Lord cry out on Golgotha?
Only language stood against
the unimaginable savagery
of gods unable to imagine pain.

"Your courage . . . Extraordinary," mumbled Diore.
He thought of inviting Dicie for a sleigh-ride,
he bent to kiss her hand but she,
she dismissed him, cowed him, with a curt
inclination. Shaking she gathered up
her reticule. She smoothed her bloody skirt.

She would not loose a cry for all the world
though her whole body howl. She swayed,
struggled to say, "I thank you, Doctor," but
it came out thickly as *Ah fank yu, Dagga* . . .
(Hopelessly, aflame with lust, he stood . . .).

True, in her pain she'd longed to roar
You base tooth-carpenter! and damn his eyes—
but this would have been ignoble, *infra dig*,
utterly at variance with what's decorous.
The doctor bowed and she bowed back to him.
I'd rather die than let
my suffering occasion a discourtesy.
What would we mortals be without propriety?
Swoopingly he held the door for her.

Precarious in hero as in suffragette,
Propriety is terror turned to etiquette.

A Fragrance of Time

1

Time is not sequential but serpentine.
Time winds in retrogressive coils.
Time monuments itself in sudden pearls,
Accretes and crests and columns travertine
Confections that turn vaporous as lace.

Time has a cabalistic face
With inward-starring facets, stalagmites
As delicate as dials;
Vials
Of stoppered venom;
Malachites
Of moments gone awry,
Gehenna's timetables, and the sly
Motherboard where all the minutes die.

Time with its plenum
Panoply—oh *la durée*!
The secondhand is scintillant in disarray.

2

For us death's moment will be crystalline,
The vein of quartz within the lode of time,
And promise of the ores of consequence.

I who have always cherished sentience
The way the May-wind-ruffled columbine
Cradles its petals as its leafstalks climb,
Am privileged to know that moment mine.

Cessation is itself a fragrance of time.

Childhood Pieties

I grew up sullen, nervous, full of tricks.
St. Paul and Milton were familiar ghosts.
I sniffed First Disobedience from the bricks
And mildewed plaster of the Lord of Hosts;
From smiling lies rouged with a crucifix;
The naphtha'd parlour and the Sabbath roasts;
The bitter bibles where the saved would mix
Apocalyptic gossip with their boasts.

I smirked rebellion and wet my bed.
Even the lustre of their sheets was fraud.
At nightmare time their Savior, leeched with sin,
Crept in beside me, worming through my head,
Embraced me, stroked me, kissed me while I clawed
The frogcold mouth of jesus on my skin.

Two Views of My Grandfather's Courting Letters

Quidve mali fuerat nobis non esse creatis?
—Lucretius

1

So here is where it all began, in these
limp prevarications and apologies!
I recognize Grandfather's courting voice too well,
its little stylistic flinches: "It would be swell
if you held me still *Your Affectionate Friend . . .*"
he coaxes and then, abjectly, near the end,
"Don't judge me so hard, Miss Juliet, despite
the jackass I made of myself last Saturday night."

I could be reading letters I wrote myself,
except that these have lain 94 years on a shelf.
These are his courtship letters which she saved,
locked in a metal strongbox, though she raved
against his "great foolishness" all her long old age.
She kept his memory bright in the soft claw of her rage.

Reading these letters I want to shout:
"Grandfather, stop! Fold up the paper! Switch out
the lamp on the supper table. Put back the quill
pen, whittled to a nib, in its snug inkwell
and tuck the unfranked stamps in the escritoire.
Cross your wedding date from the calendar.
Sidestep the meager pleasures, the great pains, to come—
the horror of a wedding bed that left you numb,
the brusque rebuffs or, at best, the grudged embrace
in conjugal obligation to prolong the human race.
I beg of you—I, wiser by nothing but distance—
confer on us, out of your countrified extravagance
and gentle hospitality
(my single memory of you,
kind whiskers and a kiss),

confer on us
with what you fail to write,
the pure gift not to be."

2

Holding his old letters I can see
how he copied each word out painstakingly—
a schoolboy polishing his copperplate.
All his hopes are still inviolate.
And I would not have it otherwise at last.
I would not soften the horror of the past.
But see, between the salvaged paragraphs,
the clumsy jauntiness, the staves and staffs,
laborious penmanship, with curlicues,
affected to impress and to amuse.

The penning of these letters on the page
fissures the time between, a saxifrage
stubbornness of promise. I have seen the root
pierce rock. I have seen the puny shoot
split stone where it flowers and endure.
Not-being-born appears so pure
but my grandfather's clumsy courtliness
shyly jollies nothingness,
embarrasses as it redeems.
I fold his letters back along their seams
and shelter them in sandalwood.

And I will say, *Write us in the book of life,*
Grandfather, inscribe us there for good.

In the Abrahamic lamp
of a Georgia twilight, my grandfather picks up his pen
and writes,

> *Dearest Juliet,*
>
> *Will you be mine?*

Cremains

I love the furnaces whose flickers turn
the citrine tincture of a tourmaline
and flack and deckle you the way gangrene
envenoms flesh with lustres of an urn.

Cremains is not a pretty word. You burn
to little clinkers with acetylene
spigots of combustion that careen
and scorch and roar till no one can discern

your earlobe from your Adam's apple or
your coccyx or your clavicle, your
left nut from your right, your nipple or
your uvula. Baby, you'll cook till you're
a soup-dish full of cinders which they'll pan
punctiliously, then pour into a can.

Little Auguries

The vast summer's distillate of cloud
rambled, thunder-proud,

while monuments of wind
bereaved my lips and left the bramble skinned.

The friendship of the ant instructed me,
I knew the honeybee's buzz-brevity.

Saluting thistles sentinelled the road:
I studied Numbers with a speckled toad.

I was tower-intoxicated, spire-
elated, the acolyte of mire-

rubies, pinnacles, abysses, mines;
what dusky zenith eglantines

Bacchic arbors of white mulberries
where patient worms, Penelopes

of satin, tend decennial looms.
I locked my summers in their silken rooms.

Expectancies of cumulus and shadowy
prefigurations of what memory

inhabited my ignorance?
An inconspicuous significance

swanned in the spotted sink
or lipped the spigot where I stole a drink

or crested the gold bristles of my manhood
or nested in my nipple where the blood

pattered like storm-drops at my sullen skin,
entreating each least clod to let me in.

I knew the rivulets of Georgia clay,
their ripe persimmon ochres, their cachet

catastrophe inscribed in crevices,
nettled my reveries, and cornices

of sandlots, stinkpot pools;
the magnesium of mackerel schools

kindled the scuffed canal
with incandescences of protocol.

Out of frog-spawn, oil-irises,
cavalcades unwound. The circuses

of polliwogs and the eyeless newt,
polka-dotted like a wind-stunned fruit,

spelled out the alphabet of wonder.
I suffered to the tutelage of thunder.

Mrs. Lazarus

Believe me, it isn't easy
Even in a king-size bed
To sleep with the living dead.
You think I can enjoy
Buttering his morning toast
When the butter's not so cold as his grey ghost?
And he's always so theatrical:
"Honey, what I've been through!"
I say, "Be a little stoical.
You could be lying in that sleazy
Mausoleum. Instead, you're here. With me."

And let me tell you straight,
It's no mean trick to stimulate
A man like that
Fresh from a grimy grave:
He needs a paramedic just to shave.
At night his chilly skin
Sweats like a ripening cheese
And little bits keep dropping off
Till the poor guy's scared to sneeze.
And the pills, the specialists, the life supports!
There's even Streptomycin in his shorts.

I don't like the way he sits and squints
Or tilts off to one side in his La-Z-Boy.
Wouldn't you think he'd have a few small hints
For the living? Instead he whimpers *Ach!* or *Oy!*
"Honey," is all he says, "it wasn't Vegas!"

All night I smell his interrupted death.
It's my own individual hell.
All night I hug his contagious
Carcass dripping with verminous breath.
I calm him as he dreams and squirms.

I who adore Chanel
Now lie down with worms.

Cradle-Song of the Emperor Penguins

Shackleton is stranded far to the north of us,
The *Endurance* stands gripped in the fists of the ice.

The skuas have withdrawn to the Cape, the leopard
Seals laze in the sun of the Weddell Sea.

Our wives have trekked back to warm surf having laid
Their eggs on our feet to brood-hatch with our blood.

Our empresses have left us to the long night of the ice.
Like goalies we cradle tense futures on our toes,

Dandling our babes against our belly skin:
All winter we will stand in a pod of palaver

Against the winds of Erebus and shield our chicks
Under pouches of down and coverlets of quill.

In the long night of the world when the green
Krakens of the aurora writhe

We fast and hold our hunger to the wind.
Our children hatch darkly. They hug our toes for life.

My tufty chicks, my fuzz-downy bairns,
I will guard you when the leopards

Of September return. I will shield you
When the towers topple into the seas of ash.

The soot of winter night is on my my tongue,
The cinders of ambushed dawn are in my eyes,

Yet I will shelter you against my belly skin
And warm your feather-weakness with heart's blood
And cradle you on the crèches of my claws.

Rowing into the Glades

I had pledged myself to rescue princesses
From the paws of ogres. I had held my sword
Between my eyes and made a solemn vow,
Like Galahad or Lancelot,
And Tommy, bold as me, had sworn the same.

Now, with sunburnt shoulders, in a seethe
Of weeds, with griping oarlocks, we
Angled our rowboat up the drainage creek.
We were following the levee engineers
Had mounded high against the rivulets
Okeechobee brims before it spills
And sidles toward the Gulf in whispering
Tributaries, lost to sight.

A kite mewed. We heard the plash
Mud turtles made careening from a log.
A water beetle surfed the troughs we carved.
The creek was deep, the water dark as tar.
The sun, sadistic princeling on a counterpane
Of plush thunderheads, squinted fierily down
And seared the lowly grasses of the shore.

Beyond a crook in the coiling stream we heard
What sounded like a woman's voice in pain.
Our princess? Tommy bent to his oar-stroke,
I redoubled mine, and so
We fairly scooted ourselves around the bend.

Ahead of us in a flurry of beating wings
A marsh hen was shrieking as it fought to fly.
We oared the rowboat closer, gingerly.
"She's caught beneath," said Tommy, then,
As I dragged the bird out, *"Jesus H. Christ!"* he yelled.
A snapping turtle hung from the broken leg
And was working its beak to drag the marsh hen down

With snake-like twitches of its hook-shaped head.
"He won't let go till it thunders," Tommy said.

I opened my hand. The bird slid under.
In sudden stillness we could hear the creek
Crawl along the bottom of our hull. We
Listened for the water as it drew
Twigs and leaves and weeds and feathers down.

We heard it suck at the muddy banks and lap
The roots of sawgrass and of bayberry.
And in the water was another sky
With a lone sun and its companion clouds
In shadowy reflection by our prow.
The black creek had swallowed all it saw.

That was the way it was for both of us
Before the world began.
Now we understood, with open eyes,
How the deeps are always dragging down what flies.

White Phalaenopsis

The protocol of orchids lies in subterfuge:
swanning petals form a curve's cortege
where slant diplomacies of lip engage

the winter-dociled bee. Such grace is made
of tasseled rhetoric, arced only to dissuade:
See how the orchid angles out of the white shade

that shrouds its calyx. Form can never lie,
we tell ourselves, although the pilgrim fly
find heaven in fragrance where it comes to die.

Is the orchid's flowering but stratagem,
mere disillusion of a diadem,
or our most tenuous Elysium?

A Salt Marsh near Truro

The wind has rubbed the dead trees to a shine
And now it flattens all the grasses down
To cowering bundles, slick and serpentine,
That twist and curtsey by the muddy brown
Brink of the salt marsh with its alkaline
Tinctures that transfigure what they drown.
The trees form a writhy circle with their brine-
Burnt branches hooked up like the six points on a crown.

Gnats and midges, the fumes of raw methane,
That oily sun going down along the Bay,
Veiled in bright pollutants, and the wind
Eroding everything to its low plane,
Convince you that this marsh of hot decay
Leaves nothing newborn that has not been skinned.

Daybreak at the Straits

> "I bow to your divinity who created darkness before
> creating light."
> —Ethiopic hymn (author unknown)

In memory of Richard Outram

1

The clouds that lie in cinnabar striations
are juggled by a nimble waterspout
too distant for significance. The dim
pink of daybreak binds the sky with dark
barely distinguishable from a darker sea.
The horizon mortices itself with chinks of rose.
What we call day is nothing more
than disintegrated darkness at the Straits.
Night bickers for asylum still
in unlaced shoes, implores the paling windowpanes
to be steadfast for dark against the light.
I am witness to the spectral provocations
daylight introduces to a vista
that all night stood
islanded by nothing but the stars.

2

Tired of the meditations on futility
that now retard my nights I walked to see
the waters of the Straits in darkness hesitate,
recoil and hover, tremble just before they calibrate
shocked sandstone, the staved cliff, the pitiable
barricades we raise against the terrible
erosions waves exact. The wind's a whittler here,
pares quartz to thinnest splinters, loves the sheer
spare sea-lathed skeletons of objects cast ashore.

It comforts me at night, a watchman of the stars
that only change by reasonable laws, to parse
the luminous degradations of the dark
as lethal light insinuates and tinges. Dogs bark
down at Rice Point, a rooster clears its throat outside.
From the cliff a cormorant topples like a suicide.

3

In the watches of the night, as the Psalmist said,
I meditate on darkness, I remember my dead.
The dark is palpable, has a silken-sash-drawn feel,
gloves the troubled fingertips with a cochineal
comfort, the way spring water laves the skin
with its brisk, plush touch. I will gather in
my hours as the darkness climbs and spreads.
It has become the ocean. Up to our heads
we bob and drift, remembranceless,
and for all we cling to spars of nothingness,
names burn their starlight on dark irises.

I feel the soul inside me, dear dieresis
that thews my breath and flesh, that separates
heart's thrusting muscle as it meditates
from all the rough heart cherishes, I sense
the supple disjunctions of the animal
threshed in the indiscernible
meshes of the element and, terrified,
crow with the cock and bark with the farmer's dog,
wriggle awake, crawl from the salt bog
of sleep unsatisfied:

on my lips and on my eyelids as the new
sun shoulders the clouds aside,
a darkness sits, intangible as dew.

A Freshly Whitewashed Room

I am sitting in the bedroom where Grandmother
Entered Calvary, where her halting breath
Prayed for the stiff-laced curtains to puff out.
I am in the sunny bedroom where she lay
So long ago, coffined in a cast
From chin to groin. How the pallid sweat
Fled from her flesh and smarted, made her
Itch with agony while I would read
The Life of Stonewall Jackson in a high
Annunciatory voice. Unknowingly I was
Her tongue of doom. The downfall of the South
Was in her bandaged bones where Stonewall bled
Tragical as Hector although not
Heel-dragged around the city gates
But fusilladed by his own smoke-staggered men.

And she would sweat and blink in the lamp
Near where I'm sitting now, though
Early sunshine pours in from the east
And the walls are freshly whitewashed
Till they fairly blaze.
Is there a sickroom sweetness just behind this new
White wall, a troubled coughing in the wainscoting
Where field-mice cache their stores? Are there echoes
Of her outcries in the dismantled fixtures?

Sometimes I think the sufferings of the old
Make heroes look ridiculous.
Sometimes I think to bring down Ilion
Was easier than to guide the bitter spoon
At medicine time to the reluctant lip.

And when the heavy book sagged in my hands
And I would nod off in the bedside chair,
"Honey," she'd say to me, "go over that page once more.
I need the fortitude of good example now."

Each caisson-jolt and bivouac emboldened her.
She grappled her pain like an antagonist.

Yet, when I read out loud to her,
It felt as if my voice
Were wearing her away
And inching her into that history
She always so clamored for.
With every word I read she seemed to me
Some punished stone an ocean works upon,
Lapping around her till it covered her
Down to the bare bedrock it rubbed away.

II.

Watchdog and Rooster

Surveying the henhouse with profound
Vigilance, taut on his tether,
Alert in sleet as well as heatstroke weather,
Crouched, eye ajar, the farmer's hound.
The rooster, however,
Accustomed to the chuckling palaver
Of his cackleophilous concubines,
Disliked the stolid silence of the dog
Who hunched there like a stinkpot on a log
And only uttered small obsequious whines
About his master's boots at supper-time.

Let us see (the rooster mused) *if this dull mutt,*
This grovel-muzzled mongrel, this bacon-butt,
This caravan of fleas, this tick-parade,
This yap-infested bozo, slow and spayed,
Let's see, I say, if this back-alley terrier,
This rumple-bellied harrier
Of shrews and voles, of polecats and hedgehogs,
Can cut the mustard with the bigger dogs!

Rooster waited till the dog, galvanized
By gazing, nodded; then, in fowlish pantomime
He stalked across the barnyard in a trot
Until he reached a strategic spot
Below the watchdog's downward drooping ear.
He then let fly a loud chanticleer
Rawp that left the stunned hound paralyzed.
The hound had never been hard
Of hearing, quite the opposite.
The clangorous crowing of the rooster, shrill pasha,
Rattled in his brainpan like a washer
On a wind-tormented pipe. He pounced.
He took the raucous rooster by the throat and trounced
Him on the barnyard till he bit
His insupportable windpipe cleanly through.

The moral of this fable still rings true:
Muzzle the watchdog when you cock-a-doodle-doo.

Episode with a Potato

I was skinning a potato when it said:
Please do not gouge my one remaining eye!
My parer hesitated. The knob of the spud
Comforted my hand-hold with its sly
Ovoid, firm yet brittle as a fontanelle,
And I much enjoyed the way its cool lump—
All pulpy planes and facettings, with a starch
Sheen that mildly slimed my fingers
(Not to mention that tuberous smell
That lingers
Like the shoulder of a clump
Of creosote bushes or the violet mildew of an arch
No triumph still remembers)—
Yes, I liked the way it occupied my pinch.

I understood at its tiny squeak
The power of potentates over the members
Of their entourages. For a week,
Whenever I passed, the potato would flinch.
Its one eye never slept.
I thought of the kingdoms it had crept
Through under the ground, spud-
Smug, amid the dust of the bones of shahs
And eunuchs, those generations of the Flood,
The Colossi and the Accursed,
The Great Hunger and the hegiras,
Telemons and ostraca and, worst,
Immense anti-archives of dirt.

It hurt
Me to do it but I scooped out its eye
And ate it and felt utterly triumphant: I
Ingested all a potato could personify.

Song for an Ironing Board

I ride an ironing board to reach the stars.
I prick it with my spurs of spatulas.
It neighs and ripples the old scorch-scars
Of its back and flanks. It whinnies
And I rear back, snorting steam.
I bridle my ironing board with wrinkled bras.
I rein it in with underwear.
How it stamps and paws its trestle!

              O many's
The dawn I've ridden forth with the gleam
Of a fresh-pressed collar and jousted with legions
Of wrinkles and mutinous pleats.
The unstarched world's Cimmerian regions
Yield to my singeing hoof-beats.

I ride an ironing board to reach the heights
Beyond all rumpledoms of wash
Where the shirtwaist alone shines triumphant.
I ride an ironing board as the iron's lights
Like clangorous horse-shoes knicker and clip.
I ride an ironing board that gallops to my lash.
It rears like Hannibal's last elephant,
Alp-traumatized, and trumpets. Its fireproof lip
Psalmodizes—

            O my war-stallion, snort-eloquent!

The Song of the Whisk

My flail demolishes
The gold of yolks;
My mesh abolishes
What it would coax.

The waterspout can frisk
While it soufflés the sea;
What's the twister but a whisk
For instant entropy?

I will erect a pinnacle
Of undulant béarnaise;
With clicketing quite clinical,
Paradisal mayonnaise.

Time as Escargot

Suppose time were not spirally and filigreed
but rather went
ambling more randomly.   Imagine
time as *escargot*, as succulence
with all remembrance curved
concentrically inside a patterned shell,
thick toward the middle then more tenuous
as newer chambers belly out above;
that is, not cyclical but
diatoming inward on itself, a
pulsing palimpsest of the ever old
configured as the new:

                                          O Snail,

the sexual residue you leave on dials,
on watch-crystals and on grandfather clocks,
your glistening viscosities of time,
your sweet slime,
patina instants, all
heirloomed in a chiton's curl.

Vacuum Pantoum

The vacuum's cannistered voracity
never gets enough; its gulf-presidium
snootsavors carpet, its mumbo-continuum
snuffles triple-ply with toothed tenacity.

I overhear the siren in the vacuum
bag that serenades as it asseverates
lint-detritus or evacuates
the peregrine residuum

that effloresces on my velveteen.
The mites in their minute imperium
are obliviated by this wolf-harmonium
whose howl's Aeolian and gabardine.

O hoover me! I hear sprawled sofas hum,
Suck on my pleats! the buxom curtains plead.
The kilim pimps the nozzle for a knead.
The louvers quiver for the slot-scoop's thumb.

The Gorgon in the Urn

I keep the family gorgon in the urn.
I don't parade it on the mantelpiece.
I keep it in the pantry behind a fern,
Swaddled by a verdigris of bacon grease.

My gorgon likes to tap against the lid
And shake her cage when I have company.
If any lady says, *Medusa me!*
I hold the urn against her carotid.

O gorgon I have urned, my gorgonette!
O clasp of adders writhing and tentacular!
Visage that incinerates the synapses!

I love the sensual ciphers of her sweat
That bead along her bronze as it collapses.
I love the lashes of her coiled vernacular!

A Dachshund in Bohemia

In memory of Hugícek

The bristle-pelted Nimrod of the rat,
Snout-partisan
Of passageways and mildewed catacombs,
Aroma-artisan,
More slink-insinuating than the barnyard cat,
The badger hound homes
In on ferrets and on errant mice.
He scruffs them in the vise

Of his unmerciful mouth and swags
Them by their neckbones back and forth.
Slack gobbets
Of fur they dangle from *jezevčík's* snout.
The brillo-coated *chlapec*
Brags
For all his yapping triumph's worth
And rasps the doorjamb till he's ushered out.

The low-slung hammock-belly of this hound
Grazes the ground.
His swizzle-brush of tail tattoos
Sousa marches when he's agitated.
It does not amuse
The long-haired dachshund to be equated
With taller dogs:
They seem precariously inflated
To our gruff terrier who completely wags
From muzzle to tail-tip when appreciated.

Jezevčík: Dachshund (in Czech)
Chlapec: fellow, guy

An Epistle from Rice Point

Nothing's gone smoothly at Rice Point. The cod
I cooked for lunch the other day had worms
And when I forked the fillet gingerly,
A fat and pinkish snout came writhing out.
My sons were sickened and quite off their feed
But I addressed the impertinence of squirms
That had enlaced our lunch with three
Brusque dollops of hot sauce. It flailed about
And finally it spoke, that worm, and said:

How dare you ladle sauce upon my head?
I am the abyssal worm that feeds
In darkness on the deep floor of the sea—
A tender coiling consciousness that breeds
In the fibers of the flesh, a wriggle-god,
A lithe mind that rivulets stupidity—
The lumpy and dull-witted race of cod . . .

"The cod was beautiful, and you are not,
You slimy eyeless annulated pest,"
I shot back and I brained it with a pot.
The worm came eeling back and now addressed
My dumbstruck sons:

                  At midnight I will twist
All through your nightmares. I'm the worm
The Gospel speaks of that will never die
And I dwell with the worm that dieth not
Inside your brainpans like a doubled fist.
Behind your foreheads where the bad dreams squirm
I'll snuggle up and peek out through your eye
Unless you eat me live.

              I took the hot
Tip of my carving knife and chopped the talkative beast
In sections, but each inch curled and writhed,

A dozen cod-worms down the platter scythed
In a sort of Todestanz combined with jive.

We are the laily worms that haunt the sea
(the wormy segments piped in harmony).
We are envenomed with the dreams of reefs,
The lobsters' anxieties, the oysters' griefs,
The lachrymose neurosis of the eel,
The torpid Weltschmerz *of the cochineal* . . .

"Enough!" I thundered and switched on the Moulinex.
"I've had enough of this annelid hex!"
I sluiced the worm-ends in the canister,
Set it to *Mince* and then *Puree*, but faster
Than I could macerate those vocal segments
Their shrill harmonics rang in yammer fragments.
A soup of cod-worms gave a grand chorale
From the kitchen at Rice Point. My terrified
Teenagers watched the worm-broth swell,
Tentacular and spittle-crested, a pale pink tide
Of liquid parasitic cod-worm consommé
Engulfed us where we crouched. I cried, *Assez!*
We wolfed the worm-soup down with zealous spoons
And mopped up every drop. The taunting tunes
Have ended now for good. All is again well
Here by the ocean down at Rice Point.

Farewell . . . Farewell.

Our Spiders

(*Naši pavouci . . .*)

Our spiders are theatrical.
Their webs are glitzy and their spinnerets
Sequin the silk they unspool as they spin.
They step processional as majorettes,
Each pedipalp held firm against each shin,
Their swivel-eyes fur-bristled and octagonal.

Our spiders are most musical:
Their eight silk-glands echo calliopes
That pedal, as they strum their tender strings,
Chromatic and Minervan melodies
That quiver on the hornet's captive wings
Like Palestrina at his most polyphonal.

Our spiders are convivial,
With intersecting webs of bonhomie;
They pool the vagaries of katydids,
They interlace to ward off anomie;
And when an aging spider hits the skids
She's invited to a lunch that's terminal.

Some say our spiders are maniacal;
That paranoia complicates their orbs;
That mutterings among them multiply
And that they snare each other with veiled barbs;
That the trapdoor spider gorged on caddis fly
Considers the tarantula fanatical.

I say our spiders are rhapsodical
Eremites of tactile syllables.
They weave a sisterhood where vocal silk
Labyrinths their mystic mandibles.
Gorgias must have sipped a spider's milk.
Like him they shimmer-loom their vocables:
Our spiders are both naked and rhetorical.

III.

Six Sonnets on Sex and Death

1

Presentiments of chaos in the telephone
alerted his left ear. He strode
over music till he found a road
angled into the fissures of a bone

—elk's bone or caribou? O Wapiti!
The Rockies with their pressure-cooker lids
were fuming when he caught up with the kids
and Mom, all rouged and wizened with graffiti.

"I once had such a tuft of names," he cried,
"a scalp of alphabets, a register
of private pronouns for my personal use!
My fingerprints keep shifting with the tide.
The droll tabloids bandy my moniker
and press me, like a turnip, for my juice!"

2

They pressed him like a turnip for his juice
which masqueraded as a precious oil.
He sweated like a basted Christmas goose.
His melancholy simmered at a boil.

They sent a dancer with red razor shoes
to trot the cha-cha on his lollipop.
They sent a leper with the evening news.
He bled laboriously but begged *Don't stop!*

This was the pietà of vacant laps,
a Golgotha of sparsely furnished rooms.
He knew the scourges of the evening stoops,
the washrag of Veronica, the sad bazooms
of Magdalenian mourners. He knew death
in every snippet of his metered breath.

3

In every snippet of his metered breath
Pleasure erected its revival tent.
Evangelists of pleasure with a wreath
of jism on their zippers would invent
cloud-copulations, cunnilingual caves,
tumescent glaciers of abiding moan,
hollows of labial comes and wallow-slaves
lathered with a lubricated groan:
orgasm-amazons with tidal spasms
slathered his lollipop with lizard tongues,
clammied his gumdrops in their sphagnum chasms
and whinnied as he wobbled on their gongs.
His dong was gorged with all their ambergris
and slithered like a walrus into bliss.

4

He slithered like a walrus into bliss
of nullity, the vacant and the void.
His all-day sucker fluttered for a kiss
but lovely nothingness was unalloyed.

Neuterness annulled his jolly knot.
The vain inane inoculated all
his tousles of temptation with a shot
and left him shipwrecked in a shopping mall

for body parts, the salvage and the wreck
of bartered bladderstones and stale catarrh.
A salesman with a demonstration dick
softsoaped him with a human-skin cigar.

All I'm looking for (he whined) *is a new scar!*
A busker twanged and picked his blue sitar.

5

A busker twanged and picked his blue sitar.
A melancholy baby in a pram
barfed a gout of frothy, fragrant scum.
A dachshund lapped it while a falling star

augured inflation and the start of war.
He wondered whether chaos would have come
in any case. His testicles felt numb.
His rectum itched and tingled like a sore.

Mortality was frisky in the lines
of telephones where drowsy mourning doves
felt final conversations in their claws
transmitted in designer valentines.

O deliquescence of our quartz-like loves!
His heartbeat hovered in two grimy paws.

6

His heartbeat hovered in two grimy paws.
He learned the sadness of quotidian
utensils, learned the glum obsidian
of office lobbies with their cattelyas
and cycads, learned to wind the gauze
of hypochondria around his median;
learned banks of exile quite Ovidian.

Only the Eberhard Faber pencils gave him pause:

cylindrical and golden as a happiness,
solar-yellow, tallow-fluted, saffron-bold.
O happiness remembered in distress!
O vaporous savor of some vanished gold!

Unwritten scripts lay tacit in their tips.
Erasers stiff as nipples rubbed his lips.

Microcosm

The proboscis of the drab grey flea
Is mirrored in the majesty
Of the elephant's articulated trunk. There's a sea
In the bed-mite's dim orbicular eye.
Pinnacles crinkle when the mountain-winged, shy
Moth wakes up and stretches for the night.
Katydids enact the richly patterned light
Of galaxies in their chirped and frangible notes.
The smallest beings harbor a universe
Of telescoped similitudes. Even those Rocky Mountain goats
Mimic Alpha Centauri in rectangular irises
Of cinnabar-splotched gold. Inert viruses
Replicate the static of red-shifted, still chthonic
Cosmoi. Terse
As the listened brilliance of the pulsar's bloom
The violaceous mildew in the corner room
Proliferates in Mendelian exuberance.
There are double stars in the eyes of cyclonic
Spuds shoveled and spaded up. The dance
Of Shiva is a cobble-soled affair—
Hobnails and flapping slippers on the disreputable stair.
Yggdrasils
Germinate on Wal-Mart windowsills.

My Grandfather's Pocket Watch

1

The filigreed watch-case clicks open and inside
I find time's intimate machinery:
The interlocking wheels' circumference,
The pin-toothed sprockets that still coincide,
Even though the little self-important melody
That marked the subdivisions of the hour
Is busted now and mute.

                    Desolate of consequence,
The pocket watch's innards look like our
Old diagrams of the Ptolemaic heavens
With epicyclical and sweet-greased spheres
—except that *Made in U.S.A.* appears
Etched on a satiny spring,
                and *George Evans*
& Son, New York, glints up from another.

2

A second-hand still whiskers the watch's face
And staggers when I shake it in my fist.

The dark dials mutter like two summer bees
Imprisoned in petals and I feel them beat—

The ratchet of a rope let down into a well:
breathless and staccato and discrete—

Each instant demarcated by a brittle click
That falters and then halts until it's shook.

The watch is dove and pearl and velveteen
Behind the dour digits of its face

Like hand-embroidered textiles or the stuffs
William Morris designed: vine-tangled arabesques

Emblematic of luxuriance and rich
Tissues drawn from some profounder life.

I twist the stem and listen for the tick
Till a tiny, startled, hurrying succession

Of twig-snapped seconds comes tiptapping out.
Each soft click is a comfort to my touch.

Lines Written after Reading Thomas à Kempis

Take comfort from your nothingness.
Inconsequence is not futility.
Get pleasure from becoming less.

Such diminution is not mimicry:
The cloud is cloudier than all cloudedness
but gets a pleasure in becoming less.

At night the skin of love becomes a sea
yet takes a comfort from its nothingness
(in consequence is not futility);

a sea that stipples at the cloud's caress
takes pleasure in becoming ever less.
Solace lies in what the lucent sea

gives up by gaining all translucency:
Take comfort from your nothingness,
Get pleasure from becoming less.

VI

UNCOLLECTED POEMS

After Becquer

The dark swallows will come back again
But we, my darling, where will we be then?
The dark swallows will come back again

And build their nests beneath the balconies.
And we, will we be less than these
Flitting wings that hide our histories?

Will we be less than these
Covert-creatures of the faithful spring?
I feel the fury of each little wing

That brings the season of our hope again.
The black swallows fly and build upon
The secret nests they left us when

They flew in autumn. When they come again,
Darling, we'll be gone,
And long forgotten, but oblivion

Will give the swallows twigs to build upon.

Big Toe

Now in my sixty-second year my two big toes
sheathe themselves in scales of calloused flesh,
are carapaced and tortugal,
each one a horny Portugal
fronting the Iberia of my foot.

The big toe's almost Alexandrian:
Callimachus might have marginalia'd
the cloudy ivory that encases it.
Look how his calligraphic lines cross-hatch
the furled scroll of the nail.
My rinsed papyrus where a reed-pen scratched
to chronicle the boulevards I've sauntered down,
my big toe is assertive as a sail
steering the felucca of my foot;
and yet, it's also cautious, a rosy snail
whose head peeps out beneath a helm of shale.
My toes are questing members, and inquisitive.
Exploratory toes! Magellan-bold!

I'm fond of plucking dustballs from the rug
between my big toe and the toe next door.
Prehensile pride invigorates my foot.
My toes that wiggle nightly under hot duvets
still semaphore
like pennants from a yacht,
although my signals always come to naught.

I scrutinize my toes in their antipodes.
They seem so stodgy and yet, these
Ambassadors to asphalt from the rest of me
Dream all night, in serried socks, of prancing footlessly.

A House in Winter

Winter sweetens my house with its scent.
What could be better than a winter-sweetened house?

In platters heaped with food and in my good roof,
In snug cushions, in drapes brocaded with dark,
I find continual pleasure against the cold.
And there is pleasure also in the courtyard pools
With their elegant pearling meander
Through gardens of grace, especially
On days when the sun-dimming clouds
Hammer against my walls
And the drain-pipes' voice, thick with slush,
Struggle to mimic the long-necked mandolins.
Then, from inside my house I watch
Other low-hanging clouds, pond-mesmerized,
Whittle slim-stemmed flagons from their subtle waves.

On evenings in my winter-sweetened house
The cup which the boy, fawn-diffident, displays
Apparels carnelian wine in winking crystal.
I adore the strands at his temples and his brow
Where musk has darkened his hair until his face
Shines out at me like the moon on a night of snow.

God has given the measures of winter and of summer.
You will not augment them with your scurrying.
Treasure your moment in this winter-gentled house!

—after al-Ṣanawbarî (d. 945 in Baghdad)

Milkweed

The milkweed with its stringent silk
Erect in October when the long blades lie
Burnished to glistening under a dwindling sky,
And the trees have the accents of things about to die,
Startled my glance, the way the tressed and milk-
Bright strands of its hidden diadem
Peep from the knobbed and gathered pods.
A field of milkweed, where each black stem
Juts from the cold earth, catches the sun
At its palest declination. Spun
Inside themselves, concealed in the husk
Of their future, the folds of the seeds
Are pleated upon themselves, are wound
The way a woman wraps a shawl at dusk
Over her shoulders. The weeds
Are populous. They column neglected ground.
Tassel and toss the smudged air of the fall.
And from a little distance the stalks grow tall
And shattered, porch and peristyle
Of some yet undiscovered ruin. Meanwhile,
At the breeze's twitch, the seeds rise
Upon the air, are lofted, puffed, they float
In the sunset, flitter like white butterflies
And inhabit all your sight. With no note
Struck they lilt on the wind, speckle the slope,
Already winter-darkened, with small swales of hope.

Murderous Roundel

My crab-like hands that bright face slashed and caught.
She gasped; I struck her twisting to the ground.
She fought my fist and died without a sound.

My forearms strained – I felt her back snap taut.
Around her neck a burst of blood I found.
My crab-like hands that bright face slashed and caught.
She gasped; I struck her twisting to the ground.

The breath within her throat my tight tongue sought;
I pressed it grinning from those lips. A clown
of blood and pain, I squeezed her breath back down.
My crab-like hands that bright face slashed and caught.
She gasped; I struck her twisting to the ground.
She fought my fist and died without a sound.

Songs of a Jug-Eared Dwarf, 3

Against Death

> "Mort, j'appelle de ta rigueur,
> qui m'as ma maistresse ravie . . ."
> —François Villon

Death, I appeal your rigor
mortis and the slow
monumental seethings of decay
that wasted my lady long ago.
You've always been quick on the trigger.
I miss her every day.

And I appeal your secrecy
that sentenced her in stealth
and reveled in her cruel decline.
You pilfered all her body's wealth
like a sneak thief – sly larceny!
I've nothing to lament her but this line.

You turned her baby blues into a gape
dull as a grouper's on a slab of ice.
Her supple skin you turned to bubble wrap.
Her sweet soft tits, twin doves of paradise,
you twisted to a mottled sausage shape.
Her lustrous cunt you turned to a sewer trap.

Where are the tiny cries she uttered when
we came together in her rosy bed?
And where are the caresses that she gave
so knowingly while giving such good head?
You dragged her amorous talents to your den
and made her darling shade your own sad slave.

Death, I do not appeal. I denounce
your decree
that has taken my lady away from me.
On my own death I hereby announce

no amnesty
for you for this infraction,
and though you pounce
I sentence you in perpetuity
to fester in your own foul putrefaction.

Songs of a Jug-Eared Dwarf, 5

To a Bird in Winter

Thicket-whisperer, you
Cherish austerity,
Your small claws blue
Beneath the raggedy

Habit of subzero
Song. And you will
Tutor me, flit-hero,
Accentual icicle,

Prophet-minor of cold-
Crunched twigs and nettle-
Skeletons; your bold
Coal-chip pupil settle

On me, where I follow
You, farther into hiddenness,
Aswarm in the swallow
Villas now left summerless.

Remembrance of the sun
Glitters your retices;
Icy octaves bangle your dun
Beak that curettes crevices.

Cauterized, chipper, astute,
You concentrate the frigid waste
In fierce fluff, my modest flute
That whistles to the holocaust.

VII

TIME'S COVENANT

This is the spring time
But not in time's covenant.

—T. S. Eliot, "Little Gidding"

Prologue

1

On Founders' Day I drove to Covenant
where my great-grandfather pitched his tent
one hundred and nineteen years ago today.

I think I hoped to travel to another time
when there was still a future, when time lay
virginal and open and each chime
of the brass-bound mantel clock above the fire
echoed into a prospect of desire.
I wanted to taste the future when it was still
all future and still ours to spend,
not the tatterdemalion remnants of the end
but the everlasting innocence of will
that places stone upon stone, brick against brick,
that hems the parlor curtains and that trims the wick
—Thermopylaes of the unyielding law
against the relentless Persians of the pass.

I drew a line in the dust where I saw
my great-grandfather's diamond etch the glass
of the bedroom window at the Tabard Inn.
I saw his histrionic and grey-grizzled chin
as he applied himself. If I could taste,
if I could taste the dust
of that entombed time, if I could just
stretch my fingertips one instant back
and track
their welling footprints in the mountain earth.
I cannot let one atom of them go.
I hold them congregated in the breath
I breathe against the windowpane
that looks out southward down the cool plateau
Earth tamps them down in cerements of rain
and I hold nothing but a lock of hair
that glitters as I twist it in the air.

2

In August when the Queen Anne's lace
bridals the meadows and the spiring vetch
crowds to the edges of the dry pathway,
before the dog days and the Perseids
punctuate the black page of the sky
with flaming commas from some galaxy
beyond our ken, and when the yellow dog
dozes in the cool clay beneath the porch,
at closing summer, when the air is damp
with small accents of fall: the ailanthus
already brandishing October fronds,
the ferns rust-tinctured, on the slope
the single scarlet of a turning tree,
and the cricket hunts more shrilly by the stoop;
in August I envisage what the past
erected to its own confusion,
ours now to elucidate: I follow
the bees, I follow the flies, and the swallow
abandons her daubs of mud beneath the bridge.

3

In August I interpret the signs leavetaking scratched
on the lintels of the houses where the lethal angels watched.
Grandfather, the gold fob on your galaxy of chain purrs
between my fingers as I fall, the windlass whirs,
sails smack and spank in the puffs of an ancient breeze.
I heard the breathing of a dead man once.
He slept below the white porch of the Inn
in the August-softened dust Oblivion
thumbprints on our foreheads when we pass.
I surprised my own amazement in the looking glass
where the resinous radiance of a chandelier
russeted the chaise longue and the chiffoneer.
Autumn lay over everything I loved.

4

In Covenant, at the Tabard as I lay,
a century later, on Commemoration Day,
I witnessed pilgrims one by one file by
and could not wipe the wonder from my eye.

Each name, new-minted, had been cut on panes
of leaded windows where remorseless rains,
where fierce frost or where the brute bald ice
could not deface nor mar the artifice
of diffident gentility
(should *pioneers* so love respectability?).

Rough-hewn timbers gave a rustic look
to the long porches and the shady nook
where travelers and pilgrims could repair
for leisured breakfasts. The central stair
lent majesty to the reception room.
There amid dusty ferns in genteel gloom
Utopians hoisted tankards of the blinking ale
and parsed the fabled future. All were pale,
lanky, strawblonde, affable and mild,
tucked roses in their buttonholes, these self-styled
"second sons," the hapless disinherited
made in the sweat of their brows to earn their bread.

I grew up to imbibe their chivalrous lies
of capsized grandeur. I too could ape surprise
at the whimsical perversity of hope.
Their future was the stub-end of the rope.

Whatever kingdom their fallen fathers dreamed
shone rustless, incorruptible, or gleamed
from the stone-skipped rivulets of humbler brooks.
All that they knew of life they'd swigged from books.

I went into the Tabard's ballroom where
superannuated hope like a veneer,

crack-glazed and scintillant, drank up dust.
Nothing is sadder than the cast-offs of the just.

The National Park
Service does what it can to nullify the dark
with stainless restorations. It smells of Mr. Clean.
And our past, calcined by acetylene,
rearises in a Disneyfied
simulacrum of a Southern Fried
synoptic gospel of what never was.
Beyond mock lintels a few real flies buzz.

5

I want to remember how our future seemed
when it was still all future. What we dreamed
when time was regnant still with possibility
in these deceiving pastures tears at me.

I've been bamboozled by what might have been.
I too was dazzled at the tacit inn.
Now I will obliterate what came between
anticipation and the demolished dream.

The Founding of Covenant

The spot commands a western view.
Here, annunciatory elmtrees colonnade
The sunrise. Good drainage is at hand.
This elevation, not a promontory,
But a modest rising of the ground
Nearly musical in effect, a mild ascension
Of the untouched earth, this virginal
Perspective which so delicately will define
Our eyes henceforth; I say, this
Particular positioning of all our hope
Here and not elsewhere, this little
Unassuming vantage where the hills
Yearn perceptibly aloft and the soil
Stands deep and black and prosperous,
Where the tributary rivulets of Eden run
Encircling our site, and there is game,
This will be our islanding, our cove,
Our harbour and our mooring, our fast
Tranquillity
          —this spot forever where the crows
comment in chorus from the optioned wood
and the rainbow-sided trout
speed the ecstatic creek.

What had been formless before took form as soon
As the Master leaned upon his spade
And struck the sudden rock. And we
Couldn't remember how the place had looked
Before it became a *place*.
Out of that almost laughable small stroke
The imminence of order stood revealed.
Plumb-lines and quadrants followed.

We created borders, not frontiers.
Frontiers possess momentum,
Borders contain and order.

The frontier associates a fixed fear
With unknowables while the border
Boundary stone or county line is dear
To our gaze. Borders are cosmogonic
As they catapult
All our yearning into memory.

Unfettered frontier has
Hugeness of amnesia,
The infinite and unremembering horizon
Which recedes behind the curtains
And proscenium of cloud, at the dwindle
Of day, when the magnitude of night
First suggests itself in the cold glory
Of Arcturus , and we glimpse across the chimney
Silhouettes, and the bravura of wood smoke
Beseeching the darkening sky,
The least infinitude our eyes can scan,
The borders of the signifying stars.

The Landscape of Covenant

Covenant sleeps encircled by twin forks
Whose waters taste of snow.

In summer
Rivulets enweb the drowsing town,
Rubbled streambeds angle the freshets down
Till they collide and coil on snagged stream-
Boulders where the glacier once
Bellied valleys out and rubbed the bleak rocks raw.
Some old upheaval riffled the stone
In decks of mica.

In winter cliffs are fanged
With ice. But on softer afternoons
The air is gentled by an almost imperceptible
Fragrance made of hay and grass and strawberries.
On the horizon you may spot
Rumblings of light
Where muffled thunder stipples the iron clouds.
You smell the rain hours before it comes.
There is a sense of peace, of laziness, but
Don't be fooled by that. A little, half-hid violence
Lies beneath the moss, beneath the damp black leaves,
And this is piquant in the summer air, prefigures
The cricket fiddlings of October in the sun-dulled grass
Or the golden opacity of gourds
Emblematic of fullness and of plenty, of surcease
And supersession.
                    The landscape here is mute
And yet articulate. Notice how pasture boulders
Punctuate the softness of the swathes of grasses,
How the knobbed stems of hacked-back shrubs rip up
Out of the loose, soft soil, or how the thistle
—embodiment of all that's bright and fierce—
palisades the edges of the lanes and ditches
in glimmering prefiguration of oblivion

that will steal all our homes and byres and stiles
away, that will fold us one day in the reclamation
of the lilacs and meld us with the long
dominion of the birches under the subdivisions.
Cadastral elms will recover their prerogatives
And shy tenacious deer will nibble the new leaves
In April, when the wind has blown
Beyond the blackened chimneys of our memory.

Covenant's twin brooks embrace the town
As though they cherished it and sheltered it,
As though it lay within two peaceful arms
Of placid water which had marked it off:
A clasp, a setting, a cove of earth and trees,
A harbor from the furies of the world,
A calm cantonment safe from lamentation.

The God who dwells within has visited
And bides among us here. The God whose voice is in
The small, soft air has touched us with benediction.
He does not ask for sacrifices, for
Holocausts of bullocks on a brazen altar. He
Is insistent in His silences. A stillness as of
Adamant emanates from Him. He pours His calm
Upon the grasses that toss in the gale,
In the bitter snowflakes that glitter above our tombs
On the hill. His calm is in the ice
That clasps the double promise of His brooks
And binds us to Him all the winter long.

Covenant is encircled by sister streams
That race from distant mountains, beyond our sight.
Our town is nourished by their secret waters.

The Crossing

1

She saw the granite hills of Newfoundland.
Icebergs impressed her with their hiddenness.
A twelve-year old in pigtails, thin and plain,
Nursing her smarting knowledge by the iron
Rail of the great ship
Plowing west.

        Grandmother, life was still
Before you then. The year was 1881.
Questions of birth and "station" already
Riddled you but in the grey
Fish-oily waters of the Grand Banks,
You saw murres and gannets, birdlime-morticed rock,
And the way the tenant birds peered from their crevices,
Row upon row in rowdy harmony
Like choristers arrayed for the grand chorale,
Seemed almost a parody of paradise:
The disparate in unison, a public peace,
The serried dovecotes of the raucous blessed,
A world where everyone had found a place.

2

As a child I peeked into her diary
Of the crossing. Now it's lost. I popped
The frail gilt lock and recognized
The classic copperplate of her dead hand.
A factual account. Spotting a pod
Of whales. The way the galley smelled.
The look of the sun at sea. Prosaically
Her every breakfast registered in neat
Detail. She had already learned to hide
All that she felt; her legacy

Was already handed down to us as if it were
Precarious porcelain, worn ivory,
The heirloom bauble of her secrecy.

3

She shepherded her secrets into Tennessee,
Those hills of abnegation, those
Refusing fields, the bitter
Immemorial drudgery. Covenant,
Tennessee, was one of those
Brutal utopias America loves:
In winter chilblains and in summer dust.
The rough-adzed privy stank and in
The sullen windowframes, Tennysonian
Bluebottles tossed without one smidgeon of
The lovely music of his desolation.

One day, her father, boilmaker's son
From Westminster with gentlemanly longings,
Cut their new surname
Into the lower pane of a parlor window
Where I spotted it a century afterwards:
MILMOW, with Falstaffian swagger scratched
Into glass, as though it could not change
Or be effaced, as though it stood
Unalterable to slander or the scuff of time.
And in January, in the stoveless
Pantry, every windowsill was rimmed with ice,
Like children's eyes with all their tears
Frozen inside them.

4

When you surprised your mother in a still,
Despondent mood, her eyes so far away,
You thought to say to her, *Maman,
À quoi penses-tu?* Knowing that if you spoke

In mother-French she was likelier to reply.
And Maman looked at you and gave a sigh,
À bien des choses, Ma petite, à bien des choses!
—the question and reply a ritual
remembered into long old age.

                       And evenings, as she
Wound her hair upon her head, I'd hear
Her whisper, *Notre père qui es aux cieux* . . .
She enunciated each pure phrase until I felt
The distant winter nights of Tennessee,
The firelight of their voices, comfortable
Hubbub, the intertwine of anecdote
And twig-crumple, the whistle of the seethed
Sap between the pondered pauses of their
Voices—ceremonious,
Half-whispering, a stately colloquy
Unremarkable except for cadences:
People talk at night so musically
To the firelight's sly accompaniment.
And if I listened to her reminisce,
The vanished voices of her sisters
Came to me again with all
The soft fiery pleasures of the hearth.

            5

I feel a tenderness of memory,
Grandmother, as though I heard your voice again
And the great sea were both our memory now.
And I will cross into your history
The way adopted children peek behind
The secrets of their surnames to discern
Darkness after darkness of the past.
And maybe it must always be just so
Whenever we touch the childhood of the dead.

Master of the Covenant

Justice for the disinherited
—that was always my aim:
to reinstate the hapless in their dispirited
state: primogeniture must maim
the soul at its root and rot
the timbers of a nation.
By birth one has, by birth one has not.
This is so manifestly an abomination.

Each man—each Anglo-Saxon—has a gift.
Tilling the soil he vivifies his soul.
Labour perfumed by leisure must uplift
And free his native genius for the role
Our Saviour has predestined him.

But must another suffer by his gain?
We have dislodged the aboriginal; the slim
Pickings of our field have brought him pain.
The souls of the freedman groan under Pharaoh's flail
And we have turned to Pharaohs in our hearts,
Despots with tender consciences who quail,
Pillaging by queasy fits and starts.

I have the highest house upon the hill.
My garden bulges with lush provender.
My granaries are stuffed to the very sill.
My seasons are strictly charted by the calendar
That tells me when to sow and when to reap.
But down by Elgin, naked wretches grub
The skimpy soil and hear their children weep.
And I am affluent—ay, there's the rub!

Shall a man who labours by his own brow's sweat
Oblige himself to succour another's need?
We've pitched our dwellings on the sweet
Pinnacles of self-reliance and the seed
Of our toil blossoms in success.

But what of unsuccess, of misery?
Do we exclude it, leave it wilderness
Or sphinx it as some riddled mystery
Not decipherable by mortal speculation?

These thoughts scratch at my mind,
And I rub at them in futile cogitation.
Are we sundered to our brothers but as wind
That flits its ignorant innocence here and yon,
Unmindful of the rich man or the poor,
Promiscuous refreshment to the one
Indifferent to the stoutness of his door?

These worries itch at me though I've rescued
A generation from uprootedness.
Still I see the hungering beggars queued
On all the roads in clamourous distress.

The supreme charity—so teaches the old Talmud
Of the Israelites—is to enable
A needy man to rise up from the mud,
To pitch foundations and to set his table
With the heaped harvest his own hands have earned.

I struggle with dilemmas that infect
My enterprise, paradoxes perned
And vertiginous, they mumble dialect
I can't quite grasp or dragoman.
My flock, by contrast, cultivates insouciance,
Is blithe and blind, an almost Saracen
Rigidity of fancy shapes their stance.
I hear them stomping "Turkey in the Straw"
Out by the barnyard, deaf to the rule of law.

Albert Milmow's Letters Home

His peregrinations took him into Uruguay,
Then to Andean mountain-towns, then on
To Panama and Yucatan. From all those
Crude caravanserais he wrote to my
Grandmother, his sister, these
Meticulous letters which I hold before me,
Their salvaged pages delicate of seam,
Their ink antiqued by distance and humidity.
And then the telegrams, the messages, the
Impulsive recitations of rough meals
Among Cordilleran starfrosts, the details,
The lean details, the tangible, quotidian
Humdrum of delays and shuntings, stopovers,
The meanness of the vistas he surveyed
Which being always elsewhere softened,
Which nomadic notebooks made nearly tolerable!

When I uncrumple these an attic odor
Rises from their surfaces. "Dear Sister
Juliet," he writes, and I read on.
It is strange to lay out letters from the past.
It is unsettling and yet conspiratorial
To read the buried messages of those
Who to our childhood seemed
Stately in their out-of-fashion clothes
And country protocols. "Now, Sister,"
He goes on, "I was most discomfited to learn
You had forbidden that young lady, whom I like,
To write to me. Please do not intervene!"
His brotherly reproof bristles from the page
Like cold air from a cave.

                        And a sharp
Presentiment of the exhaustive
Past and of his bitter future, which it holds,
In this umber, discoloured ink,

Startles me as I read,
As though his brittle letters with
Their solemn majuscules,
Were the long lassoing threads
A spider skims out over emptiness
—that they may catch some-
where, only a moment, somewhere,
scaffold us and stay, in
the flimsy structures of receding
signatures, in vanishing salutations, in
the impetuous affection of goodbyes.

Mr. Holgrove, Daguerrotypist

Do I misuse Heaven's blessed sunshine by
Tracing out men's features through its agency?
Light is the language of the Lord. With light
He limns heart-shadows. He defines the brow,
Aureoles the nostrils, tames the chin,
Allots to eyes their mica-chips of wit
Or mischief, consecrates the cuffs
From which the shady veins and sinews
Of the hands, dignified by darkness,
Issue forth. Do I blaspheme
In capturing these images?

At moments the uncleanness of my trade
Gives pause. Conferring permanence
On slivered seconds—is that not
Idolatry? Time is another name
God garbs His immobility within.
Is it not monstrous to arrest
The whirlpool of the clock?
He sentenced us to transience
But I, like Lucifer, who bore the light,
Excise an instant from its sequences
And cast it into stone with chemicals.

I have stolen something from the cataclysm
Of the hourglass, have filched a sand-grain
From the poisonous procession of the dial,
I have pinched the smallest particle
Out of the torrent. Time and Fate
Have been my deities and not the Lord
Of Time. Inescapably the crystalline
Machinery of the minute baffled me.

Around me stand the portraits of the dead
Who live still in their images. They breathe
And blink and stare, they smile or frown.

The men's beards are softened but so
Clarified by the magnesium that each hair
Shines, distinct and indelible. The women
Cupboard shadow in the folds
Of their gowns, their thrifty velvets
Hoard the glory that one instant gave
Them: even the plainest emanate
Nobility unmanacled by time.
Only the children in their sailor suits
And pinafores, only the sons and
Daughters, nephews and nieces, seem
Floating on some buoyancy beyond
Computation, though their fragile glances
Pierce the onlooker with their gravity,
like swimmers just beneath the clasping wave
Who laugh and horseplay while the toppling
Water over them unfurls its claw.

Are not my portraits votive, reverent?
Do I not celebrate the lordly form
The creator bestowed on the sons of men?
If man is in the image of his Lord
Do I not glimpse Him in the earlobes and
The cheeks, the wiry eyebrows and the widow's peaks?
Does He not whisper from the acne scars,
The very blemishes Time artifacts?
Doesn't the God of Glory thunder in
The light-tinged stubble on a young man's chin?
Do His wings of Genesis not brood above
Old cicatrices, goiters, pocks and seams,
The liver spots, the crows' feet and the jowls?
Does He not cherish secretly those jewels
Time, His whittler, gouges from our flesh?

James and Virginie: My Great-Grandparents in Daguerrotype

1: James

He gazes sideways with his fine eyes fixed
to the photographer's left. He seems to muse
wryly on the unaccustomed pose
he's meant to hold. And yet his boisterous
self—aspiring Falstaff sniffing a paper rose—
brims to the very edge of countenance.
The portraitist has snared him in a glance
Of startled, half-amused complicity,
As though he were saying to himself:

How fine I am but still, how ludicrous!
A monkey in a morning suit, my Ascot
suavely knotted, and my walking stick
tipping my witty chin; even so, how vacantly
I see the forced procession of my years!
Life is less than the ash
That will fall on my black silk sleeve
The instant the shutter clicks,
Though that dim, indivisible paring of my time
Somehow contains all worlds
That ever were. The emptiness itself
Is jocund as it fills
The infinitesimal severance of the lens.

And if you hearken to his sharp regard,
You'll hear the shutter, and its iris, wink.

2: Virginie

Life passes into folds of gentleness,
bides in the conscious pleatings of a gown,
nestles in hems of everlastingness.

Beyond the window is the sunlit town.
Beyond the town the evening-gentled hills
bide in the conscious pleatings of a gown.

And there are childhood's velvet-nestled pearls,
the fury of trousseaux, silk's hopefulness.
Life passes into folds of gentleness

that catch the coolness of October dawns.
Beyond the town's soft evening-gentled hills,
from formal labyrinths and mazy lawns

a sadness spills at sundown that still startles me
and has suffused my gaze forever now;
nestles in hems of everlastingness,

in protocols of durance, in the starched eternity
between the grave organza of a bow
and my fan, aflutter like a wing's caress.

Life passes into folds of gentleness.

"True Manliness"

Sermon preached at Christ Chapel, Covenant, Tenn.,
by the Rev. J.C. Blacklock, 1st Sunday of Advent, 190–.

My proposition is thus: *manliness is gossamer.*
How shall I deduce for you this Sabbath morn
The aboriginal manliness of God? I warn
You, Sisters and Brothers, that a cosseter
Has no true manliness but is an eunuch
Utterly, notwithstanding brassy audacity.
Mankilling Hector, I submit, under a tunic
Of oxhide and of iron was a quivering pantywaist,
His fabled courage naught but jeweler's paste.

Why is this? Can it be thus? Well, pity
Is manliness. Compassion betokens virility:
The malleable mercurial chameleon will,
Steadfast solely in not staying still,
But quicksilvering with sympathy the alien
Perplexities of other, untranslatable men!

Our Savior was a myrmidon of transformation,
Possessed the poet's adhesive imagination;
For True Manliness argues descent
Into inhospitable hearts' harsh element.
O yes, my friends, man's will is gossamer,
A puff, a flit, a piffle and a blur.
His heart is insubstantial as the thread
The orb-web-weaver slings for her homestead.
Propter hoc, I say, the manliest Messiah's he
Who swabs down pustulent limbs in the infirmary!

Imagine, if you will, the frailest flax,
Thistledown, milkweed fibers, eider wisps.
Imagine the yielding of steel, the peace of asps,
The nameless little humble daily acts
—flatirons of devotedness, not the hasps

and flanges but the swoon, O the surrender!
The infinity of God is tender.
Paradise abides in the gentle hands
Of solicitous and reverent attention,
Not in contention,
Not in the hurly-burly of the slaughter.

Ergo, I urge kindness upon you. O be kind!
For the Night is coming when man's mind
Will unravel like the yarn a kitten pulls;
When direst contrarieties
Will nullify the eons of our tossing wills.

Harbor us then, Thou ELOHIM
                                    of dim
                                              Antipodes!

Two Private Prayers of the Rev. Blacklock

1

And if I am Thy wheel, both hub and spoke,
I still must calibrate circumference,
A moveless whir of wonder like the thistle's blaze
In summer when the lanes are curled with smoke
And there is the taste of distance
In the wind and the coursed hounds laze
Under capacious porches. I will turn and turn
Like the wheel where the clay takes form
And squeezes from the potter's fingers in a squirm
Of symmetry.
I will revolutionize eternity
In the stillspin of the center where I burn.
I will begin my little perpetuity
Of praise, my mill-race rosary.

2

Lord, if I preferred the fine degrees
Of Thy justice to the antipodes
Of mercy, count it not a fault.
Judgment may not with love's vehemence assault
Thy multiple mansion, yet count me,
Count me among the just.

Count me with those who must renounce a mind
Confined
By its own infinity.
The pollen of the Law I buzzed among I reckon dust
Yet number me
Not with the worms that sting, not with the flies,
O number me among the bees of paradise.

Eden in Sepia

Age has toned their portrait to a haze
Of dimly alien faces. Whiskers predominate
Among the men, hooped and columnar skirts
Among the women. And solemn children stare
At the brief objective with black
Immortal pupils in wide eyes. Only
The terrier at center right
Would not sit still and so is now
A bristling blur with tail. These people
Have the gravity of attentiveness,
Of listening for the shutter to tease out
This instant from all others yet to be.

The portraitist has left his looming
Outline on the foreground grass, the stilted
Tripod legs, the angular flap
Of his darkcloth, and the silhouetted
Ridges of the banquet
Camera's bellows. He too is a shade
Among the shadows on the lawn.

The colonists are grouped by height, protectively
Encompassing their Master who reclines one hand,
Lamb's-wool-white through all the sepia,
On a knobby walking stick. His visionary
Eyes are hard and unreflecting as chipped flint
And his thin and lipless mouth, amid vast beard,
Has a strangely sutured look—the scar of a smile.

There is a legend to this photograph with its
Vignetted corners and its crack-glossed surfaces,
With all the names of these Christian-Socialist-Utopians
Calligraphed with a steel-tipped nib in Chinese Black.

A list of names redeemed at random from
Oblivion, even a list of names,
Surpasses elegy. How quickly the names will fade!   [277]

But if you hurry, with respectful patience yet,
You can just attend them where the voices dim,
In the last reverberations of a name
Called from a summer window or a swung screen door
One breathless afternoon when even the little terrier
Snuggled down in the yard's cool dust to sleep.

Time's Covenant (2006)

To protect my head I bought a beaded cap,
The kind Muslims wear. It hugged my skull
Like the hand of Fatima, and buoyed me up

Against the sudden crumble of a pedestal,
A toppled plinth or capsized weather-vane,
It amuleted me against the spill

Of cinders from Con Edison, against the rain
Ripe with seething acids, it was a talisman
Against stray bullets or a plunging plane.

Thou art a worm, said Virgil, *and no man.*
I was surprised to hear him citing Scripture.
The Psalms had colonized my own brain-pan

Eons before. I recognized the stricture
But couldn't help myself: my cowardice
had long been my profoundest fixture.

Dread shook me sleeping; as a child I'd piss
Myself in nightmare. And now that I am grown
I shiver when I hear the lightning hiss.

Fear is Time's spiderweb where we are blown
On ticking strands and where we count the strings
That resonate with horror of the known:

The eyes that gauge each tremor of our wings,
The box-cutter mandibles, the cruel nineteen
Who all at once present themselves as kings

Of life and death, who sing as we careen
Into the killing pillars of our opulence,
In dying accorded weird satanic sheen.

How did we get demonic and immense
In others' nightmares? Where was the line?
When did we cross it? My cap is no defense

But it keeps my brains together when blue Nine
Eleven rolls around again each year,
And I taste hot ash in sacramental wine.

Coda

Time re-invents itself. The clock re-winds.
The monuments are tricksters who quick-change.
The careful calibrations of the past
Jigsaw when we fit the pieces in,
Resist our patterns, re-array themselves.
9/11 shuffled the prism. We are lost
in reconfigured mazes that project
old assumptions on old labyrinths
blown open to the wrecker's ball.
Rats in tunnels gutted by clinicians,
We press outmoded switches and are zapped.

In Knoxville now, these melancholy scraps
Of fresh forebodings drove me to the malls,
In hellish July, across the parking lots,
Searching for Dairy Queen among the few
Shriveled maples that gave off no shade.
For a Dr. Pepper I would give my soul
I thought, ice cream and apocalypse
Possessed me, in America,
Along the Interstate. Where were the goats
I milked in the South Carolina of my childhood?
The salamanders I kept captive in a chamber pot
At the evangelical hotel? A searing
Sameness cauterized the malls, only
The acned Jesus of the Cumberland
Was dowdy, ragtag and ridiculous,
—therefore to be believed in? Bourbon
remains, all passes, even sin. Asphalt
taste of water, gasoline bouquets
blooming out of puddles, ghosts
tadpole the upturned hubcaps scummed with rain,
biscuits and grits at sunup, flapjacks
on the griddles, the final cadenzas
of the frogs at dawn beyond the propane tank . . .

Notes

For a Modest God

"A Crow at Morning." The word *hefker* is a Talmudic term meaning "ownerless," e.g., as in the case of cash found in the street.

"Mutanabbi in Exile." Abû Tayyib al-Mutanabbî, considered the greatest poet in the Classical Arabic tradition, traded on patronage at various courts in Egypt and Syria until he was murdered by robbers in 965 AD. The last four lines are my rendition of his most famous line of verse.

"The Caliph." The caliph in question was al-Hâkim bi-Amr Allâh, the sixth Fatimid caliph, who disappeared in 996 AD in Cairo and whose puzzling edicts and unconventional acts still provide fodder for scholars.

Araby

The second syllable of the name Jahâm (which means "clouds") is pronounced with a long 'a' while Adham (meaning "black") is pronounced 'Ad-ham,' with stress on the first syllable.

For some of the lore in *Araby*, I drew on Alois Musil's *The Manners and Customs of the Rwala Bedouins* (New York: American Geographical Society, 1928). For automotive details and terminology, I relied on *Auto Fundamentals* by Martin T. Stockel and Chris Johanson (Tinley Park, Illinois: Goodheart-Willcox Co., 1996).

"Jaham's Poetic Manifesto." The Arabic word *khinzîr* means "pig," an animal unclean before the Law.

"Jaham in the Autumn Rains." According to Musil, the *baharjîyah* is the pot in which the Bedouin steep coffee. The herdsman uses the call *hâb hâb* to drive his flocks.

"Bald Adham." Dajjâl is an apocalyptic figure similar to the Anti-Christ.

"Jaham Serenades a Snake." The *ka'ba* ("cube") is the cubical structure near the center of the great mosque at Mecca in which the sacred Black Stone is set and around which Muslim pilgrims circumambulate during the Pilgrimage.

"Bald Adham and Black Mary." The *'abaya* is the black, full-length garment worn by women in Saudi Arabia.

"Jaham Deciphers the Scripts of Insomnia." The names of the three short vowels in Arabic are *fatha* (a), *damma* (u) and *kasrah* (i).

"Bald Adham Falls into Heresy." Adham seems to have succumbed to the old and pernicious heresy of *tajsîm* ("corporealism") according to which God's physical attributes, as described in the Qur'ân, are taken too literally.

"Adham Overhauls an Old Caprice." The *hubâra* is that noble game bird, the bustard.

"The Jinn." The jinn are fiery intelligent beings whom God created from "a smokeless flame," according to Qur'ân 55:15. *Bunn* is Arabic for coffee bean or coffee. The *sukûn* is the orthographic sign for an unvowelled consonant.

"Ramadan." Jaham here reveals himself to be a follower of the early Sufi master Abû al-Husayn al-Nûrî.

"Jaham Praises." Jaham's lauds betray the influence of the Mu'tazilite school of theology which taught that even the most contemptible aspects of creation reveal God's justice and mercy.

"Jaham on the Difficult Beauty of the First White Hair." Al-Sharîf al-Râdî was a great Shi'ite poet who died in Baghdad in 1016. The last line of the poem is my variation on one of his verses.

"Caliph of Confusion." Iblîs (a corruption of the Greek *diabolus*) is the devil.

"Adham Atones." 'Izzat and Lât were pre-Islamic female divinities.

"Adham in the Torments of the Tomb." Munkar and Nakîr are the two angels who interrogate the dead in their tombs, according to traditional Muslim eschatology. *Barzakh* is the purgatorial limbo where the dead await the Last Judgement. Salsabîl is one of the fountains of Paradise.

"Jaham Curses." Ayyûb is the Biblical Job, honoured as a prophet in Islam.

"Jaham's Last Words." The verse the imam recites is Qur'ân 28:88.

Acknowledgements

The poems here collected in sections one to five first appeared in book form in the following:

Bavarian Shrine and other poems (Toronto: ECW Press, 1990)
Coastlines (Toronto: ECW Press, 1992)
For a Modest God (New York: Grove Press, 1997)
Araby (Montreal: Signal Editions, 2001)
Daybreak at the Straits (Lincoln, NE: Zoo Press, 2004)

Most of the poems have appeared in magazines, often in different versions. I am grateful to the editors of the following for the hospitality of their pages:

America, Antigonish Review, Arc, Blueline, Books in Canada, The Boston Review, Canadian Notes & Queries, Chelsea, Copia, Crux, Descant, Drunken Boat, eleven, The Fiddlehead, Gastronomica, The Gettysburg Review, Grand Street, Literary Imagination, The Los Angeles Times Book Review, Malahat Review, The New Criterion, The New Quarterly, The New Republic, The Other Side, The Oxford American, The Paris Review, Parnassus, PN Review, Poetry Ireland Review, Poetry Wales, Pulpsmith, The Quarterly, Salamagundi, Shenandoah, The Southern Review, The Southwest Review, The Toronto Star, Wilderness, The Yale Review.

The following poems first appeared in *The New Yorker*: "Adages of a Grandmother," "The Ant Lion," "The Caliph," "Childhood House," "Conch Shell," "Fingernails," "For a Modest God," "Garter Snake," "Getting Ready for the Night," "Grackle," "My Mother in Old Age," "Rain in Childhood," and "The Song of the Whisk." "A Freshly Whitewashed Room" was accepted for publication in *The New Yorker* in 1993 but has yet to appear. *Vitae summa brevis spem nos vetat inchoare longam!*

"Little Auguries" was first published as a broadside, in January 2003, by Delirium Press.

"The Song of the Whisk" was set to music for two voices and piano by Jed Feuer and released on the CD *twenty-one songs* (Feuermusic, 2002). "Song for an Ironing Board" was set to music for soprano voice and piano by the composer Robin Attas and recorded in performance in 2003.

"Starfish," "Skunk Cabbage" and "Origins" were anthologized in *The Norton Anthology of Poetry* (NY: Norton, 1996, 4th edition and 5th edition, 2005), edited by Margaret Ferguson, Mary Jo Salter and Jon Stallworthy. "My Mother in Old Age" was included in *The Norton Introduction to Literature* (NY: Norton, 1991; 5th edition). "Adages of a Grandmother" was anthologized in *Literature: The Human Experience* (NY: St. Martin's Press, 1997). "Flamingos" also appeared in *The Best American Poetry 1998*, edited by John Hollander (NY: Scribner's, 1998). "Rooster" was republished in *Fiddlehead Gold: Fifty Years of the Fiddlehead Magazine* (Fredericton, NB, 1995). "Skunk Cabbage" and "Live Oak, with Bromeliads" were included in *Flora Poetica: An Anthology of Poems about Flowers, Trees, and Plants* (London: Chatto and Windus, 2001), edited by Sarah Maguire. "My Mother in Old Age, "Adages of a Grandmother," "Childhood House" and "Getting Ready for the Night" have been anthologized in *Motherhood: Poems about Mothers*, edited by Carmela Ciuraru (Everyman, 2005).

ERIC ORMSBY is the author of five collections of poetry, a book of essays, and a number of scholarly studies of Islamic thought. He was born in Georgia, raised in Florida, and worked for twenty years as director of libraries and professor of Islamic Studies at McGill University. His poetry has been widely published and anthologized in Canada, the United States, and Britain. In 1992, he received an Ingram Merrill Award for poetry and in the same year was awarded the QSpell Prize for *Bavarian Shrine*. Since 2004, he has written a weekly column on literature for the *New York Sun* and regularly contributes essays and reviews to *The New Criterion, Books in Canada, The Times Literary Supplement* and *Parnassus*. He has two sons and now lives with his wife Irena, an architectural historian, in London. (photo by IRENA ORMSBY)